PAGAN
IN EXILE

PAGAN
IN EXILE

CATHERINE JINKS

CANDLEWICK PRESS
CAMBRIDGE, MASSACHUSETTS

Copyright © 1994 by Catherine Jinks

Map illustrations copyright © 2004 by Tim Stevens

First Candlewick Press edition 2004

Library of Congress Cataloging-in-Publication Data
Jinks, Catherine.
Pagan in exile / Catherine Jinks. — 1st Candlewick Press ed.
p. cm.
Summary: After fighting the infidels in Jerusalem in 1188, Lord
Roland and his squire, Pagan, return to Roland's castle in France,
where they encounter violent family feuds and religious heretics.
ISBN 0-7636-2020-3
[1. Knights and knighthood — Fiction. 2. Orphans — Fiction.
3. Religious life — Fiction. 4. Heretics, Christian — Fiction.
5. Middle Ages — Fiction. 6. France — History —
Medieval period, 987–1515 — Fiction.] I. Title.
PZ7.J5754Pae 2004
[Fic] — dc22   2003065278

2 4 6 8 10 9 7 5 3 1

Printed in the United States of America

This book was typeset in Weiss.

Candlewick Press
2067 Massachusetts Avenue
Cambridge, Massachusetts 02140

visit us at www.candlewick.com

To Rachael Westwood

"And so it was that, the Kingdom of Jerusalem having fallen to the enemies of Christ in the year of Our Lord's incarnation 1187, there was great lamentation across many lands, and the Holy Father Pope Gregory beseeched all his valorous subjects to gird themselves manfully, and liberate from the defilement of the Infidel that city in which our Saviour suffered for us. Alas, however, although many were kindled by love of the divine majesty to shed their blood, others brought down God's final punishment, making war upon fellow Christians when they should have been united in the bonds of peace. Thus did Richard of England, called Lion-Heart, and the King of France, Philip Augustus, take up the sign of the cross; and thus did they fall upon each other in discord and dissension before they had assembled their crusading armies.

"Meanwhile, in the region of Languedoc, there arose certain heretics — sons of Baal and witnesses of the Antichrist — who seduced many simple and weak-minded Christians with the abominable pestilence of heretical depravity. These vessels of Satan, the 'Cathari,' called their priests 'Good Men,' and believed that there were two creators: one of the invisible world, whom they called the benign God, and one of the visible world, or the malign God. And by clinging to these monstrous doctrines they infected our holy church, depriving it of divine favor, so that when the Crusade was finally fought, the pagan multitudes bore away the glorious palm of victory."

— Simon of Saint Medard, c. 1230

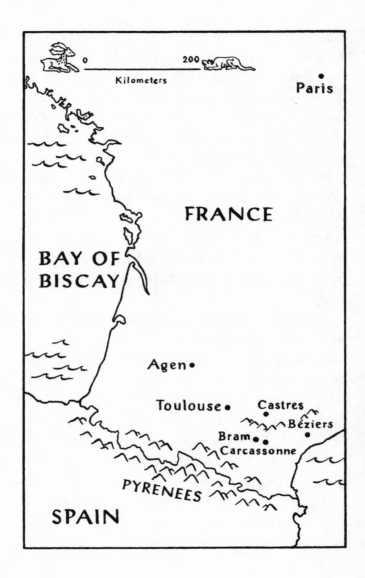

JUNE 1188

❖

‡CHAPTER ONE‡

What's everybody staring at?

All right, so you've never seen an Arab before. Is that any reason to stare? My hair's not green. My skin's not blue. It might be darker than yours, but dark skin is quite normal in my country. So I'm short. So what? I'm not that short. I'm tall enough to see over my own knees. You'd think I had a giant candle-snuffer growing out of my forehead.

Look at that fellow there, gawking away. Face like a gob of spittle, and he's staring at *me*! Why don't you get yourself a mirror, Spitface, if you really want something to stare at.

A one-armed child makes a rude gesture. Runs away as I poke out a viciously threatening tongue. No backbone, the little coward.

"Pagan." Roland's voice is cold and stern. (Doesn't want his squire eroding the dignity of his arrival.) "Please behave yourself."

"It's not my fault. What's wrong with them? They don't seem very pleased to see you."

"It's been a long time, Pagan. Six years. They may not remember who I am."

Six years. Imagine what it must be like, coming home after six years. A glance at his profile, jolting along not two arm-lengths away, as Fennel and Coppertail and poor old Brest pick a path between the puddles. (Fennel is such a lady, she can't stand getting mud on her fetlocks.) But there's no expression on Roland's chiseled face. His eyes aren't even misty. Not that I was expecting anything different: you'd see a pig become pope before you'd ever see Lord Roland Roucy de Bram in tears.

He twitches his reins, and it's time to turn right. Another narrow little street lined with pale sandstone houses, all sporting those funny peaked roofs. You don't often see roofs like that back in Jerusalem. Wooden shutters and wandering chickens. The smell of smoke and sewage. High walls. Flapping laundry. The sharp sounds of a smithy somewhere nearby.

People clustered on doorsteps, staring.

They're staring at Roland, too, of course. You have to admit he's worth a look. The golden-haired knight on his glossy black horse, with his blue eyes and wide shoulders and white tunic (well, off-white really, I haven't washed it in weeks), and the distinctive red cross on his chest. You don't often see a vision of Saint George wandering past your scrap bucket on an overcast afternoon in the middle of nowhere. It's like watching a stained-glass window come to life. People push and whisper and cross themselves. A sort of hush seems to follow us down the street.

This is really embarrassing.

"My lord!"

Aha. Someone's coming forward, at last. And there he is: a gray-haired, gray-bearded man with a wrung-out face like a dishcloth, dressed a little better than most of the people around here (who seem to be wearing tailored feed sacks) in a tunic the color of raw kidneys, and a cloak of cheese-mold blue. He looks almost groggy with shock, staggering out from under a carved stone lintel.

"My lord Roland—"

"Germain." Roland looks around. "Germain Bonace."

"My lord—God save us—we thought you were dead."

"How is it with you, Germain?"

"I can't believe it. I can't believe you're alive."

"Certainly I am alive. And well."

"It's a miracle."

"Not at all."

"We thought we'd never see you again."

Roland's beginning to get just a little impatient. You can tell by the way the muscles twitch in his jaw.

"And now I have returned," he declares. (Subject closed.) "Is my father in good health?"

"Oh—oh, yes, my lord. That is, he's feeling his age, of course—"

"And my brothers?"

"Yes, my lord. They're both well enough. . . ."

"Good." He turns to me. "Pagan, this is Germain Bonace, my father's steward. He has served my family all his life. Germain, this is my squire, Pagan Kidrouk. He comes from Jerusalem."

A mutter runs along the street. Jerusalem! The Holy City! All eyes on the skinny little Turcopole who badly needs a haircut. They're probably wondering what happened to my halo.

Yes, that's right—have a good stare. Sooner or later someone's going to come up and poke me with a stick. Just to see if I'm real or not.

"Are you on your way back to the castle?" Roland inquires. But Germain doesn't seem to understand.

"To the—?"

"We are on our way to the castle. I assume you still live there?"

"Oh, yes." The steward looks around in a dithery sort of way, as if his mind is somewhere far off, beyond the rooftops of Bram. "I've been discussing rents with . . . um . . . with Baimac—"

"Then we shall not keep you from your duties," Roland says, nudging Fennel forward. "Perhaps we'll see you this evening at supper. We must go now. Pagan?"

Yes, yes, I'm coming. The gathering crowd flinches back as we move. Toddlers scatter in all directions. Germain trails after us for a few steps, dragging a stiff knee. "Welcome back, my lord! Welcome home!" he cries in a wavering voice. Somehow it doesn't have the desired effect.

What's the matter with these people? I thought

there'd be garlands and cheering. I thought there'd be dancing in the streets. Lord Roland is one of the lords of Bram, isn't he? Don't they like their lords in this part of the world? I just don't understand.

The street opens onto a little round market-place. There's a church in the middle of it—your basic country affair—with a tower and a peaked roof and small windows. Cobbles and manure underfoot. A well. A trough. A sheep pen. A scattering of dogs and chickens and people.

Beyond it, more houses. Built in widening circles around the central square. And beyond that, the castle of Bram. Visible for miles as you approach it along the tedious road from Carcassonne to Toulouse, where everything is flat, flat, flat, like the bottom of a pan, and just about as interesting. Not quite what I expected, this castle. Not at all like the castles in Jerusalem. Those castles are big. This one's more like an overgrown road fort: a four-sided block of beige-colored stone, with the village spilling from beneath its southern flank like an accident that someone forgot to clean up. But perhaps these people wouldn't call it a village. Perhaps they'd call it a town. Two chandlers sitting on a graveyard fence are quite enough to qualify as a town here in Languedoc.

You can't see the entrance to the bailey from this point (it must be behind all those houses), but you can see the top of the keep, rising above the battlements. There are colors flapping sluggishly on a flagpole, way up high. Not that I'd personally dignify them with the name of colors. They're so worn and ragged, they don't seem to have any color at all.

I just can't believe that this is Roland's birthplace.

"Perhaps we should stop here for a moment," he remarks, glancing at the church. "Pay our respects to the priest, before we go farther."

Oh, no.

"Please, my lord." (Whine, whine.) "If I have to sit on this horse much longer I'll never cross my legs again. You'll have to chisel me off. Can't we just get to the castle and rest?"

A long, blue look from the Man of Marble. One whole day on the back of a horse means absolutely nothing to him. He could probably run from Acre to Antioch right now, if he had to. Dragging a dead donkey.

"Very well, I shall visit the priest tomorrow morning." (Hooray!) "We'll rest first. Come, it isn't far."

I'm so sick of riding. Riding, riding, riding. That's all I seem to have done for the last year. How long is it since we stayed in one place for more than two weeks at a time? Probably not since Jerusalem. Oh, and there was the ship, of course. But that didn't really count. We never stayed still on the ship, either. That was worse than riding. Up, down, up, down. God, how I hate those floating buckets of vomit.

Speaking of vomit, there's a very nasty smell around here. Where's it coming from? A tannery? A slaughterhouse? Whew! Passing the charred ruins of some unfortunate person's home. Or maybe it wasn't a home. Stables, perhaps. Or a workshop. They're lucky the fire didn't spread.

Castle walls, looming closer and closer. Dark against a pearl-gray sky. The ground rising slightly (very slightly) as the houses thin, giving way to untidy kitchen gardens, and finally to cleared land. Burned off, by the looks of it. No cover here for besieging forces. A well-kept ditch (no scrub or boulders), deep enough to bury an army in. Over it, a wooden bridge. Easy to demolish, during an emergency, especially since it doesn't seem to be in the best repair. One well-aimed rock from the ramparts and *whoomp!* No more bridge.

The horses' hooves clatter as we cross.

Someone's stationed under the big, deep arch of

the entrance. He's so small that you can hardly see him. Most of his face is obscured by a peculiar, greenish growth that seems to be a beard—unless it's a skin disease. But there must be a mouth hidden behind it somewhere, because he speaks as he advances toward us.

"State your business." (His voice is a hoarse drone, very grating.) "Halt and state your business."

It's hard not to laugh. The look on Roland's face! As if he'd cracked open a nut and found a turd inside.

"My *business*," he says, in his sharpest, chilliest, most patrician tone, "is with my family. I am Lord Roland Roucy de Bram." And he presses forward, ignoring old Greenbeard, who's got about as much authority as an apple core in a suit of armor.

Through the gates, into the bailey.

It's a fair-sized plot, but pretty crowded. All kinds of ramshackle buildings propped up against the walls. Smoke and ash drifting about. Goats grazing. And the keep, of course, towering over everything, well built, with stairs in the east wall leading up to the second story entrance. It's the only entrance that I can see: just a single hole punched through thick stone, hardly bigger than the three tiny windows sitting high up under the battlements. No one's getting in there without an invitation.

Glance at Roland. Expressionless, as usual. He's scanning the faces of the people nearby: a tall, wiry, gray-haired soldier and a drooping individual built like a beanstalk, with long, pale limbs and cold sores. They're both staring at us, speechless with astonishment.

A brief pause as Roland dismounts, moving without the slightest trace of stiffness. While his squire has to peel both buttocks off the saddle. God preserve us! I can't even straighten my knees! They'll have to break the bones and reset them. Ow! Ouch! God, my back!

"Foucaud," says Roland, carefully. He's addressing the Beanstalk. "It is Foucaud, isn't it?"

The Beanstalk simply goggles. What a pathetic sight. Looks completely boneless. Lank-haired. Unhealthy. He sniffs, and wipes his nose on the back of a hand that looks exactly like a dead squid.

"Do you remember me? I'm Lord Roland."

No reply. The Beanstalk's eyes flicker uneasily toward the soldier.

"Lord Galhard's youngest son," Roland continues, patiently. The soldier makes an explosive noise.

"Sweet Jesus!" he exclaims. "You mean you're—"

"I am Lord Roland Roucy de Bram." Cold and precise. "Who might you be?"

"Ademar, my lord, I—"

"Is my father here, Ademar?"

"No, he's gone to—I mean, no, my lord, he's not. He's at Castelnaudary, with Lord Berengar. But Lord Jordan is here." A crooked grin. (The soldier's teeth remind me of tadpoles: soft and gray and slimy.) "He's in the hall."

Roland nods. He turns back to Foucaud.

"Take these horses," he says. "You may find them a place in the stables and remove their harnesses, but don't feed them or brush them down. We shall attend to them ourselves shortly. Do you understand?"

A listless nod. Roland places Fennel's reins carefully in the Beanstalk's limp hand, and jerks his head in my direction. You don't mean that I have to touch this—this boiled lentil? His fingers feel sticky, like seaweed. Clammy. Dead. He stands there, holding all three horses, as we march toward the keep.

"My lord—"

"What?"

"Are you sure they'll be looked after?" Can't help glancing back at the Beanstalk, who seems to have

11

subsided into a trance. Roland doesn't even break his stride.

"Foucaud is my brother's varlet. I have known him for many years. He can be trusted to carry out orders."

"If you say so, my lord."

He takes the steps slowly, at a dignified pace. One hand on his sword hilt, one swinging loose. No rushing or yelling. Very cool. Very calm. Not a trace of sweat on his forehead, or moisture in his eyes. But there's a vein beating like a hammer in his temple.

And he takes a deep breath as he steps through the door.

‡CHAPTER TWO‡

God preserve us, it's dark in here! Can't see a thing except that lamp. And there's another one, way over there. On a table? Yes, on a table. You can just make it out.

Something squashy underfoot. Rushes, I suppose. Very old rushes. Probably haven't been swept out in centuries. Full of grease, bones, spittle, dog turds. There's an ominous smell in the air.

Maybe the darkness is a good thing, after all. Maybe I'd rather not see what I'm treading on.

"Jordan?" Roland, beside me, peering into the shadows. "Jordan? Are you there?"

A rustle. A creak.

"Jordan?"

Something moves beside the table. (It's getting easier to see now.) A shape seems to unfold. A hand appears in the lamplight. There's a glint of gold and a shuffle of feet. Heavy breathing from out of the gloom.

A voice.

"I don't believe it."

God preserve us. That voice!

"I don't believe it. You can't be Roland. You must be a ghost."

It's incredible. I could have sworn—he sounds exactly like Roland. For a moment I thought it *was* Roland!

"I'm not a ghost, Jordan. I have returned from the Holy Land."

"So I see."

"You're in good health, I trust?"

No comment. This is strange, really strange. Roland returns after six long years, and his brother can't even find a few words of welcome.

"Why are you sitting here in the dark?" Roland demands. Not that it's as dark as it first looked. Now that my eyes are adjusting, it's easy to see quite a few things. The trestle tables. The fireplace. The wine jug. Dingy plastered walls, very high, and black iron candlesticks encrusted with

14

tallow. Roland's brother is slouched beside one of the tables—the one on the raised dais—wearing something long and dark. There's a bird or small animal perched on his wrist.

"This is Acantha," he says. "She hasn't been trained, and we've only just taken the stitches out of her eyelids."

"Your hawk?"

"Well, she certainly isn't my mistress."

Ha, ha. Pardon me while I sew up my sides. Roland chooses to ignore this feeble attempt at humor.

"Where is Lord Galhard?" he asks. Jordan suddenly rises to his feet, and the bird on his wrist flaps its wings in protest.

"He's at Castelnaudary," comes the reply. "Negotiating a marriage."

"A marriage?"

"For Berengar." As Jordan moves into the light, you can see the family resemblance. He has Roland's long nose; Roland's blank, blue eyes; Roland's fair skin and high cheekbones. But Jordan's hair is brown, and long. He's taller than Roland, with narrower shoulders and lankier limbs. And he moves quite differently. Roland has a firm tread: his actions are always tight and controlled. Jordan slops about as if his ligaments are loose at the joints.

"I don't understand." Roland seems bewildered. "You mean Fabrissa isn't—?"

"Fabrissa died long ago. Berengar's been through two wives since then. Both dead. Airmenssens and Furneria. So now he's out looking for number four." A cynical smile. "Personally, I think he'll be lucky to find another, since he goes through wives like rope horseshoes. But then I never understood why any of them married him in the first place. Unless they actually *liked* the smell of ripe sewage."

"What happened? What happened to them?"

"Well, now. Let me think." (On reflection, his voice isn't identical to Roland's. It's slower, quieter. More of a drawl.) "Fabrissa miscarried. Furneria died of a wasting disease. Airmenssens poisoned herself."

Roland traces a cross on his chest.

"You couldn't blame her," Jordan continues. "I'd have done the same. Of course, the old lord was delighted. Three dowries, and a fourth within grasp! He's very pleased with Berengar." A sigh. "I'm afraid that *I* haven't done so well. My wife is still breathing."

Roland stiffens.

"*Your* wife?" he says sharply.

"Oh, yes. My wife. You haven't met Gauzia. That pleasure still awaits you." Jordan pauses an instant, as if expecting some kind of comment. But Roland remains mute. "God knows, I've done my best to get rid of her. I can't help it if I'm lacking in those repulsive qualities that Berengar finds so useful. It's my belief that his breath is what ultimately killed them."

"Has he—has Berengar chosen—?"

"One of the Morlans. Ada. Apparently she's about fifteen years old, so he'll probably make a nice, quick job of her." His expressionless blue eyes drift down to where I'm lurking. Spotted, damn it. "And who might this be? Your fancy boy?"

"This is my squire." (Roland, through clenched teeth.) "Pagan Kidrouk."

"Your squire?" Jordan sounds startled. "How old is he? Twelve?"

"I'm seventeen years old, my lord." No point letting him think he can wipe his boots all over my face. Look him straight in the eye, speak clearly, don't fidget. Just keep a civil tongue in your head, Lord Jordan.

"Seventeen?" he murmurs. "Is that so?"

"Pagan has been with me for a year now. He came with me from Jerusalem. That's where he was born."

"Yes, I'm not surprised. He's very dark. Turkish blood, I suppose? Funny to see you with a Turkish squire."

"Pagan is not a Turk. He is a Christian Arab. He is also a good fighter and a loyal servant."

"Mmmm." Jordan switches his gaze back to Roland. "And you, Roland. May I ask if that extraordinary costume of yours is some kind of joke? Because if it isn't, I suggest you get rid of it right away."

Whoops! That's done it. Roland's rejoinder sounds like a series of crossbow bolts hitting a stone wall. He really spits out the words.

"This is a Templar garment," he says. "And I am a knight of the Temple."

Jordan makes an odd little sound at the back of his nose. He moves right up to Roland, all loose and lazy, as the falcon flutters on his wrist.

By God, he's tall, though. Really tall.

"So that's what you call yourself. A knight of the Temple," he croons.

"That's what I am."

18

"But what does it mean, exactly? What does it involve?"

"You've heard of the Order. You must have."

"Well, yes, I suppose so. At least, I've heard that you're a bunch of Infidel-loving usurers who've all been castrated—"

"That is not true!" Roland's holding himself steady. He squares his shoulders, like someone preparing for battle. "The Order of the Temple is a military order dedicated to protecting Christians and fighting unbelievers," he declares. "We have taken vows of obedience, chastity, and humility. It is our duty to fight to the death, in defense of Christendom. In this we are following the Rule of the Order and the will of God. The blessed Bernard of Clairvaux called us the valiant men of Israel. He called us the chosen troops of God. We are not usurers. We are not castrates. We are a band of men doing our duty, according to God's will."

He pauses to catch his breath. Well done, Roland. Nicely put. Jordan's expression is hard to read.

"So you took your vows, did you?" he finally remarks.

"Yes, I did."

19

"And do those vows still apply?"

"Of course."

Jordan leans forward, thrusting his face so close to Roland that they've practically got their heads up each other's nostrils.

"In that case," he says softly, "what in the Devil's name are you doing here, you unspeakable little by-blow?"

Suddenly someone yells outside. A distant, muffled sound, but it makes Jordan jump. He falls back, glancing toward the door.

"They're home," he mutters.

More shouting, closer this time. Jordan turns away and flings himself down on the nearest bench. He starts stroking Acantha, whistling a little three-note melody. Roland stands like a statue, his face completely blank.

I wish I knew what was going on here. I seem to have lost the thread of this plot. Are we on friendly soil, or in an enemy camp? This isn't quite what I expected.

Hurried footsteps: someone's climbing the stairs. And here he is, bursting through the door—big— heavy—shoulders a mile wide. Head like a chewed knuckle of pork, all squashed and battered and misshapen, fringed by a patchy beard that's having a hard time squeezing its way through all the scar tissue on his chin.

But the nose is there. The de Bram nose, slightly pushed to one side, as if by the force of a flying punch. It looks wrong, on that face—like a steeple on a pigsty.

"Well, stone the saints!" (A hoarse bellow.) "It *is* you! I didn't believe it when they told me!"

"Hello, Berengar," says Roland. He doesn't sound overjoyed.

"What's that nun's outfit you're wearing, in God's name? You look like a dead virgin!"

"It's his habit," Jordan remarks. "He's a Templar now."

"A what?" (Is Berengar deaf? Or does he shout for pleasure?) "You must be out of your mind, you fool! Templars! Bunch of mincing Ganymedes!"

"That's not true." Roland speaks in level tones. "You're mistaken, Berengar."

"Up your arse, Roland! I know what I know." Berengar stomps across the floor, smelling of horse sweat and garlic. Still wearing his cloak and riding boots. Sighing as he lowers himself onto a bench, which creaks under his weight. "Whew! I'm

21

flattened. Where's the wine? Give me a drink, someone. You. Boy." (To me.) "Who are you, when you're breathing?"

"This is my squire," Roland answers before I can open my mouth. "His name is Pagan."

"Well, he can pass me the wine, then. Damn, but those Morlans take it out of you. Do you know they had a notary with them? A notary! I almost told them where they could stuff the bastard!"

Wait a moment. Who's this? Two more people, appearing at the door. One of them short and wiry, with leathery skin and some very impressive scars. Missing an eye, an ear, two fingers, and a big lump of forehead, as well as a large number of teeth. The sword at his waist is almost as big as he is.

The other man is built like Berengar: broad, heavy, powerful, tall, but not as tall as Roland. He has a big black beard and a bald patch. Shaggy eyebrows. Tombstone teeth, slightly brown at the ends. An inflamed complexion. Wearing a lot of leather and fur.

He stands there, dragging his gloves off. Everyone falls silent.

Could this—? This couldn't—

"My lord," says Roland. And he bends his knee. Lord Galhard.

22

Oh, yes, that's him all right. It's got to be. You can tell by the way he's suddenly the center of attention. He clumps across to the high table, picks up Jordan's cup, and drains it. Pours himself another. Drains that, too. Everyone watches . . . watches and waits.

"Just passing through?" he says at last. His voice is like the sound of gravel crunching under the wheel of an overloaded wagon. Like the sound of bones being ground up in a stone pestle. Never in my life have I ever heard such a chilling voice.

"Yes, my lord, in a sense." Even Roland seems subdued. "I am here to request your hospitality. For myself and my squire. According to your will."

Galhard grunts. He lowers himself carefully onto a wooden bench (saddle sores?) and sticks out his right leg. "Boots, Joris," he mutters. The little man with one ear comes scurrying over to haul his boots off.

"So, you're here to request my hospitality." A pause. "Wearing what, may I ask?"

God preserve us. Here it comes. Roland straightens his shoulders and sticks out his chest.

"My lord, this is the cross of the holy order of the Knights Templar." His voice is clear and firm. "I am a Templar now."

"Is that so?" (Ominously.) "Then let me tell you that as a Templar, you're not welcome on these lands."

"My lord—"

"Don't interrupt me!"

(Gulp.)

"Your friends the Templars seem to think they have some God-given right to poke their collective noses into my affairs," Galhard continues. "They call it 'the Peace of God,' or some such rubbish. But I suppose you know all about that."

"No, my lord, I—"

"Then you can ask your friends about it. Meanwhile, if you want my hospitality, you can take that shroud off and keep it off until you leave. As my son, you're welcome. As a Templar, you're not. Is that clear?"

"Yes, my lord."

"And if you don't have anything else to wear, you can ask Jordan. He's got enough damn clothes to fill a moat."

No comment from Jordan. No comment from anyone. Roland lowers his gaze and studies the dust on his riding boots.

I wish we hadn't come, now. If you ask me, this was a mistake. A big, big mistake.

✝CHAPTER THREE✝

"It's a monster, I tell you. Enormous. Isarn saw the pellets. Long and fat, with rounded ends. You don't see a juvenile leaving traces like that."

"You don't see any stags leaving traces like that so early in the year. They must be old."

"Up your arse, Jordan! Do you think Isarn doesn't know a fresh turd when he sees one? There were flies all over it!"

"Then it must have been left by something else."

"Jordan's right, son. I never saw a stag's droppings that weren't as flat as a cow pat, before Saint John's Day."

This is too much. I mean, I've digested my dinner in some pretty rough places, but never during a conversation about excrement. Can't these people talk about anything else?

"What color were the pellets?"

"Brown, my lord, dark brown."

"Should be black, by that stage. Jordan's right. They must have been left by another animal."

Unless the whole discussion is some sort of trick. Perhaps it's designed to put other people off their food. Provided, of course, they've actually managed to get any food. You'd have to be built like the Temple of Solomon if you wanted your fair share of salted herring at this table. It's a fight to the death for every last scrap.

"What's the matter, Pagan? Why aren't you eating?" Roland, beside me. He looks so strange in that outfit. I don't think I've ever . . . no. It's true. I've never seen him in anything but white: either one of the Order's ankle-length winter robes or his white campaign tunic with the red cross. And now he's sitting there in a blood-colored woolen surcoat trimmed with jade-green silk, worn over a tunic of embroidered purple linen that's just a little too long and a little too tight across the shoulders. It makes him look different, somehow. It makes him look younger. Less responsible.

"I'd eat if I had anything *to* eat, my lord." Softly,

so that no one else can hear. "You didn't tell me I had to come to supper fully armed."

Roland knits his brow and casts a look around the table. It's a pretty disgusting sight. Berengar, muzzle down, gobbling like a pig at a trough. Galhard, with chewed-up bits of food spilling from his mouth as he discusses the unique characteristics of wild boar droppings. Jordan, sucking his greasy fingers. And the other squire—Galhard's squire. What's his name? Aimery. Aimery Sais de Saint-Felix-de-Carcassonne. (What a mouthful.) Moodily dissecting a dumpling with one hand as he props up his chin with the other. Not much of a prospect, that fellow. Sullen and spotty. Hope no one decides that we ought to be friends. Just because he's a year or so older than I am doesn't mean we're natural allies. It simply means he'll try to beat me up at the earliest opportunity.

Aha! And here comes the next course. That delicious smell, like a trumpet blast, announcing its arrival. The Lord is gracious and full of compassion: He hath given meat unto them that fear Him.

Roland bends his mouth to my ear.

"Don't try to grab any of this," he murmurs. "You haven't the weight. I'll get enough for both of us."

"No, my lord!" (Quietly, Pagan, keep it down.)

"Please don't do that. They'll laugh. They'll say I'm weak."

"You will be weak if you don't eat something. I'm not having you starve to death because of my family's table manners."

God preserve us. I can just hear the remarks. No one else gets served except Jordan's wife, and she's pregnant. Glancing over to where she sits, at the very end of the high table. What an unhappy woman. Limp black hair, hollow cheeks, gnawed fingernails. The circles under her eyes are so dark she looks as if she's been punched. Maybe she *has* been punched. It certainly wouldn't surprise me. Jordan behaves as if he can't stand the sight of her—a feeling that seems to be mutual. He drops every handful of food onto her bread like someone throwing dirt into the grave of a deadly enemy.

And she doesn't even look at him when he does it.

Galhard belches, loudly, as the spicy smell drifts closer. There it is! An enormous, steaming pot, carried by a man who has to kick his way through a pack of drooling dogs before he can even get to the table. He has big, beefy arms, and a jaw like

28

the head of a battle axe. As he edges past our seat, the smell of cesspit mingles with the smell of pork. Whew! Is that *him*? Catching Roland's eye.

Somebody ought to throw that man into the nearest running water.

"At last!" Berengar exclaims. His gaze is riveted upon the approaching pot. Muscles tense. Stomachs growl. And *clunk*.

The pot hits the table.

What a mess. What a joke. Everyone diving, lunging, grabbing, pushing. Dogs whining. Food everywhere. The sound of fingernails scraping on iron.

Roland seizing my bread. Forcing his way through the press of bodies. (Go, Roland, go!) Emerging, breathless, with a puddle of green stuff.

"What's this?"

"Seasoned pork."

"But it's *green*."

"It's dyed with parsley. There's nothing wrong with it."

If you say so, my lord. Personally, I think it looks like the kind of thing you'd clean out of a horse's box every morning. But then, when you think about it, so do most of the people around here.

Gauzia rises abruptly and leaves the table. No one asks her what's wrong. In fact no one even looks up from the food, except Roland—and he's got something more important to think about. I can tell by the way he takes several deep breaths before speaking. Obviously he's decided that it's time to break the news.

"My lord," he says, turning to Galhard, "you may have wondered why I decided to return to Languedoc, after all these years in the East."

"No." Another spray of greenish pork particles. "Can't say I have."

"Well, I have come here on a mission. An important mission. It concerns the fate of the Holy Land."

A grunt.

"You must know that the Infidel Saladin has conquered the kingdom of Jerusalem," Roland continues doggedly. "He captured the king and destroyed the king's forces. Only a few coastal cities remain in Christian hands."

"Yes, someone did mention it. Can't remember who."

"For this reason, many people around the world are preparing for battle. They are preparing to arm themselves against the Infidel, and return to the Holy Land to reclaim the kingdom that was lost.

Just as they did a hundred years ago, on the First Crusade."

A sudden surge of noise from the other end of the hall. Some sort of fight going on. Old Greenbeard. What's his name? Pons? Sprawled across a tabletop, trying to strangle his neighbor.

"Oi!" (Berengar.) "Keep it down, over there! We can't hear ourselves think!"

Think? *Think?* Is that what you call it? The rest of the garrison closing in, trying to smooth things over. But Pons breaks free. Starts banging his victim's head against the table.

"Pons." Galhard raises his formidable voice. "Siddown."

"But—"

"Sit down!"

Pons sits down. He knows what's good for him.

"I don't hold with fights over food," Galhard growls, to no one in particular. "It ruins the digestion. Now what were you saying? I lost track."

"My lord, I have spent the last six years fighting to defend the kingdom of Jerusalem against the Infidel, according to the will of God." Roland is choosing his words with care, laying each one in its proper place like a man laying mud bricks. No mention of the Templars, I notice. "My duty now," he continues, "is

31

to seek support in this quest to reconquer the Holy Land. That is why I have returned to Languedoc."

"Surely you're not looking for support around here?" Jordan interjects. He sounds amused.

But Galhard turns on him. "Shut your mouth, Jordan. This isn't your concern."

"My lord, it's true that I came to ask you if you would consider playing a role in this campaign." (Roland adopts a neutral tone.) "Many kings and princes will be leading it. The Pope has given his blessing, and has promised absolution and remission of sins for all those who take up the Cross."

"The Pope can eat stewed scorpions and die," Galhard retorts. "Why should I go rushing off to the other side of the world and leave my lands unprotected?"

"Someone could stay. Jordan, perhaps."

"*Jordan?* I wouldn't trust Jordan as far as I could spit a pip!"

Loud laughter. Even Jordan smiles. But Roland's face remains expressionless.

"There are many good reasons for going," he says quietly, "just as there are many good reasons for staying. It will be a campaign blessed by God—"

(Galhard snorts.)

"—and it will also be the greatest adventure of our age."

"I'm too old for adventure, son. I just want a quiet life."

More laughter from around the table. Roland's studying his hands. I can feel how tense he is, just sitting beside him: every word is being forced out, with the most colossal effort, like a yolk being blown through a pinhole in an eggshell.

"Last time . . ." He stops; hesitates; proceeds. "A hundred years ago, when our Christian forces first conquered Jerusalem, many lords of Languedoc won themselves great wealth and honor. They became the rulers of the Holy Land."

A long pause. Now *that's* hit the target. They sit there, eyes glazed, chewing reflectively. Aimery's carving a picture in the table with his knife.

"I suppose it could be worth thinking about," Galhard finally agrees. "But everything depends on the Viscount. If the Viscount goes, and all his vassals go with him—"

"I tried to speak to the Viscount on our way here," Roland interrupts. "When we were in Carcassonne. But he'd gone to Castres. It's my intention . . .

that is, I had thought to visit the Count of Toulouse, as well."

A sudden explosion of mirth. Berengar pounds the table. Jordan chokes on a crust. Even Aimery manages a sour kind of grin.

"Raymond of Toulouse!" says Galhard in his gravelly voice. "What makes you think Raymond has time for such nonsense? Raymond's got his hands full, son!"

"What do you mean?" Roland sounds puzzled. "I don't understand. Has something happened?"

"You mean you don't know? You must be walking around with your ears full of wax!" (Berengar.) "He's in a head-to-head with Richard Angevin!"

"Of England?"

"Of England. And Poitou. And just about everywhere else, the bastard." Galhard scowls as he stuffs the last remnant of pork into his mouth with one hand. "We heard the news at Castelnaudary."

Richard. Richard. This would be the eldest son of King Henry, I suppose. The big blond one. The fighter. I've heard about him. Isn't he supposed to be joining the Crusade?

"It started around the Feast of the Holy Cross," Berengar breaks in gleefully. "They say Raymond carried off three merchants of Richard's allegiance. Castrated them."

"*What?*"

"Or blinded them. We don't know exactly." Galhard waves the boring details aside. "So Richard raids the Count's lands, and makes off with Peter Seillan."

"Peter Seillan," Jordan adds softly, "is Raymond's deputy in Toulouse."

"So then Raymond turns around and throws two of Richard's knights in the guardhouse." (Berengar takes over the story again.) "They were on their way home from a pilgrimage to Compostela."

"And now Richard has invaded Raymond's lands in Quercy," Galhard finishes.

Well, what a mess. And I thought Richard was supposed to be such a noble character.

"This can't be true." Roland seems dazed. "Richard is preparing to leave for the Holy Land. With King Philip of France."

"I wouldn't bet on it."

"He can't abandon the Crusade for something so—so petty. So futile. It's impossible."

"What do you mean? There's nothing petty about it," Galhard snarls. "If some snot-nosed

35

Count of Toulouse castrated three of *my* mill-owners, I'd stuff his balls with minced onion and fry them in oil."

Yes. Well. I don't suppose there's any doubt on that point. Roland falls silent, as Galhard shifts restlessly on his seat.

"Speaking of minced onion . . ." he adds. *"Oi! Bernard! Is there any more supper, or am I going to have to stick a spit up your arse and roast you?!"*

Poor Roland. Poor thing. It's hard to believe . . . no. Not hard. It's *impossible* to believe that this is Roland's family. I'd sooner believe that a unicorn would hatch from a serpent's egg. Look at him, sitting there. Like a swan in a swamp. Cheer up, my lord. You did your best. You asked them to join the Crusade, and now it's up to them to decide.

Personally, I think we'd all be a lot better off if Galhard Roucy de Bram shut himself up in this castle and never set foot outside it again.

‡CHAPTER FOUR‡

So this is the kitchen. All smoke and grease. And dogs, of course. I hope none of those dogs is for dinner.

"Yes? What do you want?" That must be Bernard. Roland said he was fat. He looks like a great, quivering heap of stomachs with a head perched on top. Even the head seems to be nothing but a collection of sweaty red jowls.

"Are you Bernard?"

"Yes. Who are you?" His voice is a high-pitched, bad-tempered squeak.

"I'm Lord Roland's squire. I need tallow and rose oil, to polish some harnesses." Hold up a harness, just to make sure he understands. "Do you have any?"

"Of course I do. Segura! No, don't sit there, boy. I'm using that."

Well, pardon me for breathing. His flab jiggles as he pounds away at something (hazelnuts?) on a wooden board. The kitchen table is big enough to stage a battle on. Long, dubious, brownish things dangle from strings tied to the rafters. What could they be? Look like petrified dragon turds.

A woman enters through the southern door. Bit of a human wreck, poor thing. Practically hump-backed; gray-haired; chalk-faced. All loose and floppy around the chest.

"Segura," Bernard squeaks, "where's the leather polish? I never know where you put things."

Without a word she shuffles toward a set of shelves that run across the entire length of the room. They're piled high with pots, spoons, knives, string, onions, garlic, dried herbs, flour sacks, dish rags—you name it. I suppose she's his wife. Pulls down a green-glazed bowl and examines its contents.

Passes it to me.

"Thank you." Just two simple words, but she behaves as if I'd given her the crown of England.

Stands there with her mouth open, gawking. "Do you think you could give me a rag, as well?"

With an effort she drags her eyes from my face, and starts rooting around in a corner. Pushing the dogs aside as they jostle for position. Bernard throws down his wooden stick.

"I'm going to have a word with Germain about those eggs," he says.

"It won't do any good," she replies. Crossly.

"When I want your opinion, I'll ask for it."

Cheery place, Bram. Full of love, life, and laughter. Bernard lumbers out the door, puffing and blowing like a bull on a cow's back. His wife hands me a shred of gray fabric that looks as if it's passed through somebody's bowels.

"Oh. Thank you."

Better than nothing, I suppose. Now, where shall I sit? Not too near that big vat of frothy gray stuff. It might be quite harmless (whey, perhaps, or dishwater), but then again it might not. The stool near the fireplace looks all right. Nobody seems to be using it. And nothing seems to be on it.

Get out of my way, dog, or you'll be wearing your teeth out the back of your head.

"There! There he is! I told you!"

Look up. It's Isarn. I recognize that lazy eye from

supper last night. Belongs to Berengar, doesn't he? Oily hair and sharp elbows. A sly, unsavory smile. Always cracking his knuckles.

Beside him, the kitchen hand with the battle-axe chin. The one who smells like very old fish guts. They told me his name, too. Not Isarn. Is—Isold? No. Isoard! That's it. Isoard. He sneers at me and folds his arms.

"Yes," he says, "that's the one."

"No wonder I didn't notice him last night. He's a midget."

"Not only that, he's an Infidel."

By the beard of Beelzebub. Not again.

"If you're talking about me, I can assure you that I'm not an Infidel. I might have Arab blood, but I'm a baptized Christian. My mother was also a Christian, because she put me in a monastery when I was very small. So don't call me an Infidel. There are lots of Arabs in Jerusalem who are just as dark as me, and they're all better Christians than you are."

Isarn snickers. Obediently, Isoard proceeds to make various farmyard noises that might be mistaken for laughter. But you can see he's waiting for Isarn to explain the joke. At last Isarn obliges.

"Listen to the way he talks!"

"Oh, yes, that's right, he talks funny. Ha ha ha."

God give me patience. No point wasting breath on those morons. Dip my rag into the bowl. Scoop up some grease. . . .

"His skin's a funny color. It's all muddy. Don't those Infidels ever wash?"

"Wash? They wash about five times a day. They're always taking hot baths. With perfume in them!"

"They sound like a bunch of eunuchs."

"They're not eunuchs. But you know what they are? They're circumcised!"

"Huh?" Look at that pus-bag Isoard. Doesn't even know what "circumcised" means. Suddenly someone else comes in. It's Greenbeard. "Ademar wants to see you, Isarn," he drones.

"Ademar? What does he want?"

"I don't know, but he says he wants you now."

Must be the only soul on earth who does. Isarn points at me.

"Look, Pons. See that Infidel over there? That Infidel doesn't have a foreskin."

"Now listen." (That's just about as much as I'm going to take.) "I *do* have a foreskin, I'm *not* an Infidel, and would you kindly remove your malodorous great mouths before someone mistakes you for kitchen scraps and throws you to the pigs with the rest of the garbage!"

Takes a while for the insult to really sink in. Isoard goes red. Pons goggles. Isarn bears his teeth.

"Think you're pretty clever, don't you?" he hisses.

"As a matter of fact, I'm not alone in that opinion."

"Well, I think you're lying." He takes a step forward. "I think you *are* an Infidel. And I also think you've been circumcised. Isoard!"

"What?"

"I've never seen a circumcised penis before. What do you say we take a little look?"

Isoard grunts and moves around the end of the table, covering the left flank. Isarn sidles off to the right. Damn, damn, damn. Why is this always happening to me?

"Back off, bog-brain."

"Listen to him whine."

"I said *back off!*"

"You're not scared, are you? He's scared, Isoard."

Loud laughter. Pons isn't playing: he's decided to watch. Segura? She's retired to a safe distance. No help there.

Get up, Pagan. Slowly, now . . .

Isarn lunges. *Smash!* Gets a big bowl of tallow, full in the face. He staggers as Isoard lurches forward. Grab the stool! Throw it—*crunch!* Off his elbow. Time to go, Pagan. Run straight through the middle and—*hup!* Onto the table. Pons at the other end. Isarn grabbing from behind. Jump to the right, but Pons is surging forward—*ouch!*

Knees hit the floor.

"What's going on here?"

Jordan. Oh, no.

Someone releases my collar.

"Lord Jordan." Isarn's voice? Look up, and it's Jordan, all right. Wearing a long, blue robe and carrying a hooded falcon on his wrist. Bit puffy around the eyes.

Late night, by the look of it.

"What do you think you're doing, Pons?" he says gently.

"N-nothing, my lord—"

"What's that on your face, Isarn? Dog spit?"

"No, my lord, it—he—that boy threw grease at me."

"Did he, now? And why was that? Because he didn't like your far-from-endearing face? Or was there another reason?"

"No, my lord—I mean—I don't know—"

"You don't know? Somehow I find that hard to believe." A prod from Jordan's leather-clad foot. "Get up, boy. What's your name? Pagan?"

"Yes, my lord, Pagan."

"Is it true? Did you throw grease at my brother's varlet?"

"Yes, my lord."

"Why?"

"Because he was going to attack me. He wanted to see if I was circumcised."

"He's a liar, my lord." Isarn. Whining. "That's a dirty lie."

Jordan looks around. He spies Segura.

"Were you here?" he asks.

She nods.

"Is this boy telling the truth?"

Another nod. Isarn begins to protest.

"That stupid old woman—she's practically blind."

"Listen to me, Isarn." Jordan places his free hand on Isarn's shoulder. "If you're so terribly interested in genitals, I suggest you concentrate on your own pathetic set."

Whomp! A swift kick, straight to the groin. Isarn buckles.

God preserve us.

"There," says Jordan. "That's given you something to think about, hasn't it?"

No reply from Isarn. Just a terrible groan. Jordan turns to Isoard, who flinches.

"Get out. You, too, Pons. Out!" Another kick for Isarn, this time a light one aimed at the ribs. "Get out of here, you disgusting creatures. All of you!"

No one waits to be told again. Isarn crawls. Isoard staggers. They're gone before you can draw breath.

Leaving Jordan to finish his business.

"I need meat for my bird," he announces, without even looking at Segura. He seems more interested in me. She scurries off to serve him while he stands there, gazing down that long, familiar nose.

"Roland tells me you can read and write," he says at last.

"Yes, my lord."

"Where did you learn to do that?"

"In a monastery, my lord."

"A *monastery*?"

"I was brought up in a monastery. In Bethlehem."

Pause. He moves over to the table, dusts off some flour, and seats himself.

"Then why aren't you a monk?" he says.

"Because I ran away."

"Ah, of course. You ran away. When did you run away?"

"When I was ten years old, my lord."

"I see. And where did you go then?"

"To Jerusalem."

"To your family?"

"No, my lord, I don't have any family. I never knew my father, and my mother didn't want me."

What's all this about? Is it some kind of trick? He sits there, stroking his falcon with one long finger.

"You can't have joined the Templars when you were ten years old," he murmurs.

"No, my lord, I did that when I was sixteen."

"And before then? What did you do before then?"

"Nothing, my lord. At least nothing to be proud of. Just garrison work." And that's all I'm going to say, Lord Jordan. Because I don't trust you. You're a cut above the other two, and you certainly saved my skin, but you're dangerous. I can smell it. There's something hidden underneath.

"Well, I'm sure that whatever you did, it was interesting." A smile creeps across his face. "No one else in Bram can read or write, you know. Not even the priest. And none of my family ever had an education; we're all just as illiterate as Roland is. Of course, we used to have a chaplain who could read—he lived here in the castle—but he's dead now."

I'm not surprised.

"He was my mother's chaplain." Turning to look at Segura, who's sidled up with a long, ragged piece of bluish flesh. "What's that supposed to be?"

"It—it—"

"What do you think I've got here? A lymer hound? Cut it up, quickly."

"Y-yes, my lord."

"And I want small pieces. Small. Understand?"

"Yes, my lord."

"Stupid woman." He shifts his gaze back to me. "My mother had three books, which were part of her dowry. The chaplain used to read them to her. He had to translate them, of course, because they were all written in Latin. Two of them were gospels, but the other was a historical book. William of Malmesbury's *Chronicles of the Kings of England*. My father burned the gospels, but I kept the history. I was never very interested in it when I was young, although I do recall one extract about a witch who was carried off by the Devil when she died. I was read that particular story in the hope that it would encourage me to mend my wicked ways." He smiles a little. (Now I know why his stare is so compelling. He hardly ever blinks.) "But lately," he adds, "I've been looking at the pictures,

47

and they make me wonder what the words mean. Do you read Latin, by any chance?"

"Yes, my lord. Latin is what I read best."

"Then perhaps you could read me this book, sometime?"

"Yes, of course."

"It would give me something new to think about."

Segura is still frantically sawing away at the sinewy meat, with a knife as big as a battle axe. Jordan rises, and the falcon on his wrist flaps her wings a few times before settling. The bells on her legs tinkle as she moves.

"She's a beauty, isn't she? A real diamond."

"Yes, my lord."

"Exotic, too. She's not a local." He fixes me with that blank, blue look again. "A bit like you, in fact. Have those witless animals bothered you before?"

"No, my lord. This is the first time."

"Well, if they do it again, don't hesitate to call me."

"Thank you, my lord." (Are you serious?) "But I don't think they'll be that stupid."

"My dear Pagan, you must never underestimate the stupidity of the people around here. I assure you, it never ceases to surprise. Ah, at last." Once more Segura has approached him, this time with the meat chopped up and carefully arranged in an earthenware bowl. He takes it without a word of thanks.

"I daresay you must feel like a walking spectacle at the moment, but it won't last," he continues. "And even while it does, you mustn't let such ignorance affect your peace of mind. Remember that no one here has much to do, so they'll stare at anything out of the ordinary." He moves to the door, treading carefully on noiseless feet. The dogs don't follow him: they keep their distance, their eyes on the bowl he's carrying.

Suddenly he stops and turns.

"Don't forget about that book," he adds. "I'm ready whenever you are. Or whenever Roland decides to allow you a few spare moments. He's obviously much too busy praying to do anything for himself."

Now what's that supposed to mean? Watching as he walks away, his falcon lurching and flapping on his wrist.

If you think I'm going to stand and smile while you make remarks like that, my lord, you're very much mistaken.

49

CHAPTER FIVE

Casting an eye around the bailey. No sign of
Roland here. No sign of anyone, very much. Just a
scattering of people watching Aimery tilt at a
chain-mail hauberk, which he's stuck on a pole and
stuffed with straw. (I suppose you could call it a
quintain.) Riding a rather nice gray gelding that's
much too small for him. Doesn't old pimple-face
ever do anything else? I'm beginning to think he
must take his lance to bed every night.

No sign of Isarn, thank God. Or Pons. Or
Isoard. Who's that on the stairs? Germain's wife?
That's it, Germain's wife. Tayssiras. I recognize the
bosom. Lifting up her skirts to feel for each step

with her foot. Tiny feet, she has, for a woman of such ample curves.

"Hello, Master Pagan!" Dimpling at me. Nice to see a happy face around here. "I hope you're well this morning."

"Hello, Mistress Tayssiras. You're looking very pretty." She is, too. All dressed up in a rich, red gown over something long and pink, her glossy hair wrapped around her head and pinned into a silk net trimmed with silver.

"Thank you." Dimple, dimple. "I'm just off to visit my friend Dulcia, in the village. She has a new baby."

"That's good." (Good that it's over in the village. God preserve me from drooling babies.) "Have you seen Lord Roland?"

"Lord Roland? I think he's in the hall."

Aha! Thought so. "Thank you, Mistress Tayssiras. I hope you enjoy your visit."

Waiting politely until she's cleared the last step. Wonder how Germain ever got himself a wife like that. She must be thirty years younger than he is. Nice-looking, too. She's left a trail of perfume behind her, strong and flowery. Teasing my nostrils all the way up the stairs.

From inside, the sound of someone's voice.

"Teats like a breeding sow. What an armful! I almost got smothered."

Berengar. Telling filthy stories again. Through the door, and here he is. Lounging at one of the hall tables (which hasn't been cleared since last night). Here's Ademar, too, cleaning his fingernails with a sharpened stick. Fancies himself as a bit of a lady's man, does Ademar.

The air feels thick and heavy.

"Well, well, if it isn't the little Turk." (Berengar.) "Where do you think you're going?"

No trace of Roland. Maybe he's upstairs. I can't imagine he'd stay too long in this den of squalor.

"I'm—I'm looking for Lord Roland, my lord."

"Well, he's not here."

No, I can see that.

"I think he's upstairs," Ademar suddenly remarks. "I saw him talking to someone. Joris, perhaps, or Pons."

You mean Joris can actually *talk*? I don't believe it. Skirting the northern wall, past the entrance to Galhard's sleeping chamber. A glimpse of the great, wooden bed, hung with grubby curtains and piled high with twitching, snoring dogs. Galhard's there, but not Roland. Past the locked pantry door, and into the stairwell. Gauzia's sitting halfway up the circular staircase, dressed in what looks like a night-dress: a loose, yellowish garment laced up the sides. Her eyes are shut. Her hair's uncombed.

Don't tell me she's fallen.

"Lady Gauzia! What's wrong?"

She opens her eyes and scowls. "Go away," she says.

"But—do you want some help?"

"Go away! Get out of here, you filthy Turk!"

All right. If that's the way you feel. Squeezing past her enormous belly; sticking close to the wall. These stairs are so narrow, there's barely enough room for two people to pass each other. Whoof! What's that stink? Don't tell me someone's been pissing on the stairwell.

And suddenly here's Foucaud, carrying a pile of soiled crockery. What a hive this place is. No privacy anywhere. Just one big stack of people, getting on each other's nerves.

"Foucaud! Have you seen Lord Roland?"

Sniff, sniff. Why doesn't that beanstalk learn to blow his nose, like a normal person? "Yes, I have," he says.

Pause.

May God give me patience.

"Could you perhaps tell me where you saw him?"

53

"In the chapel."

The chapel? "What chapel?"

"It's over there." He waves a soggy hand. "At the far end."

"Thank you."

Leaving the Beanstalk behind. Just a few more steps, and here we are in Berengar's room. Long, spacious, and messy. Full of dogs and bridles and maces and swords and boots and belts and chewed bones and candle wax. An open chest, stuffed with clothes. A narrow bed piled high with furs. A palliasse on the floor . . .

That's Isarn's palliasse. And that's him in it. Moving past quietly, so as not to wake him up.

Must still be suffering from the effects of Jordan's boot in his groin.

The door on the left leads to Jordan's chambers. I wonder if he's in there. (Maybe he and Gauzia had an argument.) The door on the right is the one I want. Takes you straight through to our room—and whatever lies beyond. Still a bit of a mess, this place. Junk piled up in the corners. Broken barrels, bits of glass, worn-out shoes and spare firewood. No one's found Roland a proper bed yet: it's terrible to see him sleeping on the floor. Our clothes still rolled up in our saddlebags.

And someone's been going through them again. The thieving pus-head didn't even bother to put everything back properly. Damn these maggots, to hell with their prying fingers! They've already taken Roland's ivory comb—what else do they want? If I catch the person who's doing this, I'll hang his guts out to dry.

"My lord?"

No answer. Where's this chapel? It must be on the other side of the linen closet. That would mean going straight through the far door and turning left when you can't go any farther. Funny sort of place to put a chapel. But then I'm surprised they've got a chapel at all. I bet nobody uses it, except Roland.

Across the next threshold, and through a little room stacked from floor to ceiling with tablecloths: tablecloths and blankets and something that's either a campaign tent or a very old tapestry wall hanging. Looks like moth heaven to me. Squeezing past a cedar chest to get to the only other door in the room, which is thick and heavy and encrusted with black iron bolts and rivets. It opens onto a smallish chamber with a single, shuttered window.

Peering around in the dimness, trying to make

out where I am. Whitewashed walls. A carved crucifix. Two rows of squat, stone columns propping up a network of groin vaults. An altar. An altar cloth. Two candles. And right in the center, somebody's tomb.

White marble, by the look of it. About as high as my shoulder. With Roland leaning against one stony flank, his head on his folded arms, which are pillowed on a marble stomach.

"My lord?"

He looks up.

"Are you all right, my lord?"

"Pagan . . ."

Don't tell me he's been crying. No. Of course not. No, his eyes aren't even red.

"I've finished cleaning the harnesses, my lord. And someone's been going through our bags again. Is there anything we can do about that?"

"I'll ask. . . ." He sounds almost groggy. What has he been doing? "You've finished the horses, I suppose."

"And the riding boots. And all the equipment. And I've put the blankets out to air. Let's just hope that no one takes them."

"I'm sorry, Pagan." Wearily. "There's nothing much I can do. This isn't a good place."

You're telling me. "My lord?"

"What?"

It's hard to find the right words. How can I possibly explain? I wish he wasn't wearing that crimson thing. He doesn't look like Roland anymore.

"My lord—" (Please help me.) "My lord, I—I feel like a freak."

"You what?"

"I feel so out of place here." Swallowing hard. "Ever since we left Jerusalem—but here, especially—everyone seems to think I'm an Infidel. They treat me so—the way they talk—everyone is always staring."

"They're worthless, Pagan. Ignore them."

"But how can I? They even laugh at the way I speak. Don't they understand that everyone talks differently? In Jerusalem pilgrims came from all over the world, and nobody laughed at the way *they* talked."

"Pagan, listen to me." He reaches out and puts a hand on my shoulder. Bending forward a little, so he's looking me straight in the eye. "Most of the people here are without God. They steal, they lie, they are violent and cruel. Do you think that anyone who serves God would feel comfortable here? I certainly don't."

(But that's not the point.) "My lord—"

"My mother was never happy here. It was she who had this chapel built." His hand leaves my shoulder, coming to rest on the smooth, cold slab of white marble. "She wanted me to be a priest, you know."

No, I didn't know. How interesting.

"She tried very hard, but my father—Lord Galhard—he wanted his sons to be fighting men. Tough fighting men. Everything we did . . ." A pause. His eyes glaze over as his mind wanders back to some half-forgotten memory. "There was a game we used to play at the table," he murmurs. "We'd put our heaviest boots on, and kick each other's legs until someone gave in. It was called Bone, that game." Another pause. "My father usually won."

God preserve us. Sounds like a load of laughs.

"When did your mother die, my lord?"

"Six years ago." His hand moves across to a carved ankle, draped in stony fabric. Squeezing it gently. "This is her tomb. It was made before she died. A sculptor came all the way from Lyon. My mother was a northerner herself, you see."

So *this* is his mother! Climbing up on the pediment, to take a better look. Standing on tiptoe,

58

craning my neck. She's lying with her head on a lion's back, her hands pressed together in an attitude of prayer. It's an amazing piece of craftsmanship. You can even see the pattern at the edge of her robe and the shape of her knees under the folds of fabric. She has a long, serious face and— yes! The nose! The famous de Bram nose!

"Look, my lord! She's got your nose!"

"My nose?"

"I was wondering where it came from. Your father doesn't have it."

He fingers his nose and smiles, but doesn't comment. There's a spray of fresh violets sitting on her chest.

I suppose he picked them himself, this morning.

"She—she must have been a very noble and beautiful woman, my lord." What else can I say? But for some reason it doesn't seem to go down too well. Instead of smiling, he frowns.

"Yes, she was," he replies. "Has someone been talking about her?"

"No, my lord." (Would that be a problem?) "I worked it out for myself. Because you certainly don't take after your father."

This time he's speechless. Opens his mouth. Shuts it. Opens it again. His expression shifting from disapproval to amusement to sorrow to embar-rassment to frustration. At last he finds his voice.

"Thank you for the compliment, Pagan, but I must ask you not to make such remarks. They are disrespectful."

Oh. Right. It's like that, is it? "If you say so, my lord."

"I'm sorry that things have been so difficult for you here. But you mustn't be discouraged, because I doubt that we'll be staying for much longer."

Really? "You mean—"

"I mean that my father will soon be making his decision. And I'll be very surprised if he takes a crusader's vow."

Well, I won't argue with that. If you ask me, Galhard's more likely to end up in a nun's habit than on a ship to Jerusalem. What I want to know is why we even came here in the first place.

"It's odd how you forget," he continues, running a hand along his mother's chilly, chiseled arm. "I thought that—if I came back—I've been away so long, you see—"

"Lord Roland."

It's Joris. Old One-eye. Haven't heard him speak before. His voice is a rusty creak: probably lost half his throat, along with everything else. What a mess that man is.

"Lord Galhard wants you, my lord," he announces. "You must come to the hall at once."

He doesn't wait for an answer. Just turns to go. But Roland calls him back, using that frosty, Commander-of-the-Temple tone that's always so effective.

"Wait, Joris." (You impudent scum-bucket.) "Has something happened?"

"Visitors, my lord."

"What visitors?"

"Women, my lord."

Women? *Women?* Well, that's informative. Roland removes his hand from his mother's impassive likeness.

"Tell my father we're on our way," he says.

‡CHAPTER SIX‡

They've lit some rushlights in the hall. If you ask me, it wasn't a wise thing to do: now you can see that the tables need scrubbing. You can also see how dirty the walls are, all covered in grease and smoke stains. They must have been white, once, with red flowers painted on them. Now they're a grayish, mottled color—the color of Galhard's feet.

He's taken his boots and stockings off and appears to be trimming his toenails with a hunting knife. Berengar's still lounging near the hearth with Ademar and a few dozen dogs. There isn't a single woman to be seen.

. "My lord?" says Roland.

Galhard grunts. He's concentrating hard. (Must have toenails like slabs of whalebone.) Berengar speaks for him.

"It's this Good Woman again," he remarks. "Esclaramonde Maury. We thought you might be useful."

"Good Woman?" Roland's totally mystified.

"She's got a couple of farms up near Saint-Martin-la-Lande. Right next to our forest there, at Lavalet. Bunch of nuns or something. Lord Galhard gave her the rights to any wood she could collect, in return for harvest gifts and jurisdiction."

"You mean an abbess?" says Roland. He's still confused.

Galhard snorts.

"I told you." (Berengar.) "It's just a couple of houses. With a few men working the land. She's nothing but some merchant's widow from Carcassonne."

It still doesn't make sense to me. But there's no more time for explanations: someone's already walking up the outside stairs. You can hear the sound of a woman's voice, low and urgent.

Galhard drops one foot and picks up the other. He's about as welcoming as a fist in the face.

63

"Here she is," says Berengar. "Come in, Mistress! Don't be shy! We're not going to eat you."

The poor woman advances over the threshold, less reluctantly than you would have expected. She's wearing a long, black robe and a black scarf around her head. Her face is as white as sea salt, but her eyes are very dark. She's even smaller than I am.

"My lord Galhard," she says, falling to one knee. A chip of Galhard's toenail flies through the air. "May I speak, my lord?"

"I'm listening."

"My lord, it concerns your forest at Lavalet." She has quite a deep voice, for such a small person. "There's been an assault, my lord."

"Go on."

"A man called Garnier has been assaulted. He is a Good Man who works the land belonging to the house where I live. He lives in the house next to mine, and he was in the forest with his son, collecting wood. But someone else was there, too."

Galhard looks up. Now he's interested.

"Who?" he says.

"I believe it was a man called Clairin. He is a servant at the Abbey of Saint Jerome. I believe he's been cutting wood in your forest."

"I knew it!" Berengar exclaims. "Didn't I tell you? We ought to go down there and—"

"Shut up, Berengar. Continue, Mistress."

She doesn't seem at all uncomfortable. In fact she's very self-possessed. Surprising, when you consider how young she must be. Twenty? Twenty-two?

Awful to think what she might be kneeling on.

"My lord," she says, speaking clearly and firmly, "Garnier's son Estolt was working by himself when he heard shouting. He returned to his father and found Garnier with the man Clairin. Clairin had struck Garnier on the head with an axe." Her voice trembles slightly. "It was a terrible wound, my lord. He has not yet revived, as far as I know. Estolt seized the axe, but Clairin fled. So Estolt carried his father home on our cart." She waves a hand in the direction of the stables. "We have brought the axe with us, my lord."

Galhard nods. He seems to be thinking. The woman waits patiently as Berengar shifts about on his bench.

"Why did you come here?" Galhard says at last. "What do you want me to do?"

"My lord, the forest is your forest. What happens there is your concern."

"Damn right it is." (Berengar, airing his opinions again.)

"I believe that this man from the abbey has been plundering wood," she continues. "Garnier has seen him there before, but not with an axe. Perhaps you want to take this matter up with the Abbot." She hesitates. "I think that justice should be sought for Garnier's assault. He may not live, my lord. If he doesn't, his family deserves some kind of recompense."

"Recompense! I'll go down to the abbey and find this Clairin and pull his guts out through his nose!" Berengar roars. He slams his fist down on the table. "I'll tear him up and feed him to the dogs!"

"No. Please, no violence." The woman lifts her head. "I don't want any violence."

"What you want, Mistress, doesn't interest us at all," Galhard snaps, in a voice that would flay a dead camel. He looks at Roland and jerks his head. "Come here."

Roland moves forward. A glance at me, over his shoulder. (Stay where you are, Pagan.)

"This is my youngest son, Roland. He's just come back from the Holy Land. He used to spend a lot of time at the abbey, so he knows his way around there." Galhard sneers, displaying a collection of fangs that would put any of his lymer hounds to shame. "I haven't set foot in that God-box for fifteen years, and I'm not about to start now. I know I wouldn't be able to control my temper. That's why I'm going to send Roland to speak with Abbot Tosetus."

Can't see Roland's face, so I don't know how he's reacting to this announcement. Probably hasn't even raised an eyebrow. He rarely lets anything show, especially in public.

"The Templars are always at me about peace levies and the Peace of Toulouse and the Peace of Béziers and peace this and peace that," Galhard continues, in a threatening way. "Interfering with my private business. Trespassing on my land. Fancy themselves as peacemakers, for the right price. So I'm leaving this little matter to you, Roland. As a knight of the Temple, it should be the kind of thing you're trained to deal with."

Roland bows. Can't really do anything else, I suppose.

"Take this woman with you," Galhard tells him. "Wear your fancy outfit. Make that bastard sweat. I want to know how much wood he's taken, and I want compensation down to the very last twig."

"My lord—" The woman dares to interrupt.

Galhard swings his head around and glowers at her. "What?" he barks.

"My lord, the Abbot will not talk to me. I doubt if he'll even let me through the gates of the abbey. He has very strong feelings about my . . . my establishment."

"I don't care if he spits blood and dies at the sight of you! You'll be there under Roland's protection, and Roland is my son. If he can't get a hearing, then the Abbot will be hearing from *me*." He waves his knife, almost cutting her nose off. "If you go now, you should be there before sunset."

And that's a dismissal. But Roland hesitates: there's something on his mind.

"My lord—"

"What?"

"My lord, our visitor has already traveled a long distance today. Perhaps we should let her rest, and begin in the morning."

"Roland"—sarcastically—"our visitor is probably a lot tougher than you are. Now get going, before I put you on a mangonel and send you by air, with a large rock tied to your ankle."

Impossible to argue. Roland throws another look at me (this time it's a summons), and we head for the door. Berengar yells a few words of encour-

68

agement after us. "Tell the Abbot that we found his balls when we were out hunting truffles! Tell him we'll trade them for Saint Agatha's teats, if he's got them!" A burst of laughter follows us out.

How embarrassing.

"You're very kind, my lord," Esclaramonde remarks as we march down the stairs, "but I'm not tired. I came on a cart, not a horse. And I wasn't driving."

Roland stops. His voice is cold and hard.

"Who came with you?" he queries.

"Estolt came with me." She points across the bailey to where a solid wooden farming wagon is already attracting the attention of our resident dogs. One of them appears to be pissing on a front wheel. "I think he went to the kitchen, because he was so thirsty."

She's not at all intimidated by Roland's Man of Marble expression. In fact she looks him straight in the eye as she speaks. Somehow, although he towers above her, he doesn't make her look small.

"I will send your friend home on the cart," he announces. "And I will borrow one of my father's horses for you to ride. Or would you prefer a mule?"

"I can ride a horse."

"Good." You could break rocks on every word he's uttered. What's the matter with him? There's something going on here. I can smell it. "Go and collect your belongings. Tell your friend that he must return without you. We will meet you at the stables as soon as we're ready."

"Yes, my lord."

"Try to be quick. We have a long way to go."

She nods and hurries off toward the kitchen. Roland turns on his heel. Retraces his steps. Something's really bothering him.

"My lord—"

"Hush. Later. Tell me later."

Back into the hall. They're still laughing: Galhard and Berengar and Ademar. But Galhard stops laughing when he sees Roland.

"I thought I told you to get out," he snarls.

"My lord, this woman—"

"You're trying my patience, Roland."

"My lord, it seems to me that this woman is a Cathar." (A what?) "Is that true, my lord?"

"Don't ask me."

"But if she's a Cathar, then she is a heretic. And if she's a heretic, then there are many things that you should consider. My lord, the Viscount of Carcassonne was excommunicated ten years ago because he was a heretic. If you allow free entry of heretics into Bram, then you may be accused of the same crime—"

"Roland." A breathy hiss, like the voice of a serpent. "Let me make one thing clear. I'm not interested in what you think. What happens in Bram is my business. Now get out of here before I lose my temper."

Come on, Roland. (Tugging his sleeve.) You don't want to kill yourself. Can't you see that there's no point in arguing? It'll just lead to confusion and ill will, not to mention dismembered body parts. Let's go and pack—you said we had to hurry.

I almost have to drag him upstairs to our room.

"My lord? *My lord?*" (Wake up, Roland.) "Are you going to change? Lord Galhard said he wanted you in uniform."

"Yes—yes, I'll do that."

"And your hauberk, my lord? Will you wear that too? It'll look more impressive."

Doesn't even hear me. Staring into space.

"My *lord.* Shall I pack your hauberk, or will you put it on?" He blinks and seems to shake off his trance. Looks around at the piles of rubbish.

"I'll wear the hauberk, but you can pack the rest

71

of the chain mail," he says. Right. Good. Now we're getting somewhere. Perhaps if I start with the shoulder pieces.

"Pagan." His hand on my arm. "Listen to me for a moment."

Looking up. What's wrong? Have I done something?

"Pagan, I don't want you talking to that woman."

"You mean Esclaramonde?"

"She's a heretic. A Cathar. She's dangerous."

"But she's the size of a thimble!"

"Her ideas are dangerous. She could do you a great deal of harm. Please, Pagan." He really seems worried. Almost scared. "I don't want to leave you here, but I will if there's any risk that you'll talk to this woman."

"Well then, I won't talk to her." (If it will make you happy.) "I still don't understand, though. What's a heretic? Some kind of murderer?"

"A heretic . . . a heretic is like a wolf."

"A wolf?"

"I mean—no—a heretic is outside the church."

"Like an Infidel?"

"No, not quite." Poor Roland. He doesn't seem to know exactly *what* a heretic is. "Heretics follow

72

the Devil. They say they are Christians, when they're not. They are outside the church."

"Like the Byzantines?"

"No, not exactly—"

"Like the Jacobites?"

"No, I—no—at least—" A pause. "I don't think so."

"How do you know she's a heretic? She didn't say anything."

"I—it's hard to explain." (That's pretty obvious.) "There have been heretics in Languedoc for years and years. You see them everywhere—thousands of them. They have set up their own church, with their own bishops and priests, because they say that the true church is the whore of Babylon. Their priests wear black robes. Black robes and sandals. Did you see that woman's sandals? Imagine a church that allows a woman to be a priest!" He runs his hand through his hair.

"I don't know much about heretics, Pagan. All I know is that they are wicked and wrong. Abbot Cyprien told me so, many times. He was the Abbot of Saint Jerome. He told me that the Cathars' heresy is a very ancient one, which came from the East, and that it has spread among the lords of this

73

land because they don't have to pay any money to the Cathar bishops. He's dead now." Roland shakes his head, slowly. "I wish he were alive. It would make things much easier. I don't know what the new Abbot will think if I arrive on his doorstep with a heretic."

Well, I do. I can tell you exactly what he'll think. He'll think that you've converted her back to the true faith. "My lord, no one's ever going to believe you're a heretic. If that's what's worrying you."

I mean to say, what a joke. Even someone with half a brain would see at a glance that Roland couldn't possibly be a heretic.

Whatever a heretic might actually be. I'm not sure I'm clear on that one yet.

‡CHAPTER SEVEN‡

God, how I hate monasteries.

It's the smell that really gets to me. That awful smell of old books and incense. And the silence, like being shut up in a tomb. And the echo of shuffling feet down long, long corridors. I hate the way no one ever runs in monasteries. I hate the way no one ever shouts. It's all whisper, whisper, whisper, like a bunch of dead leaves in the wind.

Speaking of wind, it's drafty in here. That's another thing I hate about monasteries: they're always as cold as a crypt. Cold and miserable. I remember what it used to be like at the Nocturnes service, before sunrise, when your knees used to freeze to the floor and your breath came out in great, white clouds when you sang.

A bell rings nearby. That sounds like the end of Vespers.

"Maybe he's had an attack of dysentery."

"Pagan—"

"Well, why is he taking so long, then?"

"Be quiet, Pagan, please." Roland lowers his voice. "Someone might hear you."

"Really? I hope so. Because I'm beginning to think that they must have forgotten us."

No comment from Esclaramonde. She's been very quiet. In fact she's hardly said a word during the entire trip. Not that she's had very much in the way of encouragement: Roland can't have addressed six words to her since we left Bram. I daresay he wouldn't have talked to her at all, if I'd been allowed to speak to her myself.

This is so stupid. I mean, she's obviously about as dangerous as a dead duckling.

"It'll be time for supper soon. Do you think they'll bother feeding us? Or will they just let us sit here and starve?"

"Pagan."

All right, all right, I get the message. Sudden

snort from Esclaramonde. Look around, and she's vigorously rubbing her nose with her cuff.

Was it a sneeze or a laugh, I wonder?

"Lord Roland. *Deo gratias.*" Hooray! It's the rescue party. And that must be the Abbot. An old, old man, leaning on a stick. Totally bald. Skin like the membrane beneath the shell of a hard-boiled egg.

Behind him, a handful of monks in black robes. You can hardly tell one from the other. (All monks look the same to me.) One of them carrying a towel and a basin.

"My lord Abbot." Roland rises. "May God bless you for your gracious hospitality."

"God's blessings on you, my son," the Abbot gurgles; he's got some kind of nasty chest complaint. Roland stoops, and they exchange the kiss of peace. Up comes the basin; a splash of water; the Abbot wipes Roland's hands with his towel. *"Suscepimus Deus misericordiam tuam in medio templi tui,"* he mutters without much enthusiasm. Cough, cough, cough. That old man should be in bed.

"This is my squire, Pagan Kidrouk," Roland announces. "He came with me from Jerusalem."

A rustle of wool as the monks react. Here we go again. Everyone stares at the funny-colored foreigner.

"He is welcome," the Abbot croaks.

"And this is . . . this is Esclaramonde Maury."

No response from the Abbot. He doesn't even look in her direction. Some of the monks cross themselves.

"We are here on a matter of some importance," Roland continues. "It concerns my father's lands at Lavalet."

The Abbot nods. His fingers are stiff and swollen. "Then we shall speak, of course. Are you refreshed? Have you eaten?"

"No, my lord." Roland shakes his head.

"You haven't?"

"No, my lord."

The Abbot turns, his jowls quivering. One of the monks whispers in his ear. They both look at Esclaramonde.

"Yes, I see." (Cough, cough. That Abbot sounds like a pair of old bellows with water in them.) "Well, later perhaps. If you would just come this way, my lord? There is a reception room, through here." He waves his crippled hand at his attendants, who scatter like crows. Only one remains, a sour, jaundiced monk with scaly red patches on his skin. It must be his job to keep the Abbot from falling over. "This way, Lord Roland, if you please."

Shuffle, scrape, shuffle, scrape. It's painful to watch the old man limp along. Passing from the dim, gray anteroom into an equally dim, equally gray, but slightly larger reception room. Some kind of mural painted on the wall, up near the ceiling. Cold stone tiles underfoot. A selection of mismatched furniture: folding stool, high-backed chair, stone bench, carved ebony table. A gilt cross hanging above the window.

"Please be seated."

The smell of cooking food, somewhere. We must be near the abbey kitchens. Or maybe the Abbot has his own kitchens. Back in the monastery of Saint Joseph, we used to have a special wing for the Abbot and his guests. Just to make sure that none of the monks talked to visitors.

Looks as if they might have the same arrangement here.

"My lord Abbot, this is a very joyful occasion for me." (Roland, getting things started.) "Before my journey to Jerusalem, I spent many happy days under the roof of your most venerable and holy foundation. I have also listened many times, with the most profound humility and respect, to the words of your predecessor, Father Cyprien, may God have mercy on his soul."

"*Gloria Patri.* He was a grievous loss to us."

"I can imagine. A most worthy servant of Christ, most dutiful and devout. His guidance was always a blessing."

"He that handleth a matter wisely shall find good; and whoso trusteth in the Lord, happy is he."

"Amen."

Ho hum. What a bore. Glance at Esclaramonde: her head is bowed, her hands are folded. She looks exactly like a nun.

"Lord Abbot, you must forgive us for this intrusion, but my father felt that we should settle a certain matter that affects many people, including yourself." Roland's treading carefully: there's no emotion in his voice at all. "It concerns a man called Clairin; I believe he is a resident of this abbey?"

"We have a servant by that name."

"Only the one?"

"As far as I know."

"And does he often enter my father's forest at Lavalet, to collect wood?"

The Abbot stiffens.

"Never," he declares. "This abbey has no right or claim to any produce from that land."

"Then I must tell you that Brother Clairin appears to have dishonored your authority, and assaulted a free man known as Garnier of Lavalet, while collecting wood in my father's forest."

There. That's done it. No more compliments. No more courtesies. Now we're getting down to business.

"I find that hard to believe," the Abbot retorts. "Have you any proof of such a thing?"

"My lord, this woman lives and works in the same community as the injured man. She has seen his wounds. She has spoken to his son, who witnessed the assault, and who identified Clairin." Roland gestures toward Esclaramonde. "I believe there may be grounds for some sort of inquiry."

The Abbot's face puckers. His jaw begins to move. His fingers twitch on the head of his cane.

"I do not agree," he snaps.

"My lord Abbot—"

"This . . . this *woman* . . ." (Scowling at Esclaramonde.) "This woman, or should we say demon, is a false witness and a foul perverter of the truth.

Her tongue is polluted. Her house is the way to hell. This woman is like the whore of Babylon, drunk with the blood of saints, and no good Christian should bear witness to her filthy deceits."

Uh-oh.

"My lord Abbot—"

"Go back to your father, Lord Roland, and tell him not to defile himself, but to shut his ears to the profane counsel of Lucifer, whose teeth are spears and arrows, and whose tongue is a sharp sword."

"I am not a liar." Esclaramonde leaps to her feet. "I am not a liar. I am not a false witness. You are unjust." Her dark eyes blazing, her voice sharp and strong. "You are like Saul, when the evil spirit came upon him!"

God preserve us. The Abbot tries to speak, but his words are swallowed by a fit of coughing. Esclaramonde turns to go. Roland grabs her arm and pulls her back.

"Sit down," he hisses.

"You are like Jezebel!" (The Abbot's found his breath again.) "You are like the beast with seven heads and the names of blasphemy on them! You have defiled this house with your corruption and filled this man's ears with lies!"

"I will not stay here!"

"No, you will *not* stay here. You will leave the abbey grounds at once. You are an evil woman, not welcome in this holy place."

And off she goes. As fast as a flea. "Pagan! Stay with her!" Yes, my lord, that's just what I was thinking. She's so hampered by the length of her skirts that she doesn't get far before I've caught up. Barely manages to clear the first corner.

"Wait. Hold on. Don't run away, Mistress." Catching her arm. "I know it wasn't pleasant, but he's probably senile."

"He is unjust!"

"I know, I know he is. And incontinent, too, I'll bet."

She can't help laughing. It's a reluctant kind of laugh, but it's a laugh.

"I was foolish," she mutters. "They were only words. That was very foolish."

"Oh, I don't know. I think you were pretty restrained. If it had been me, I would have shoved his walking stick up his left nostril."

Another smile. But it doesn't last long. She's obviously a serious-minded person.

"I'm sorry," she says. "I've ruined everything. What should I do? Is there anything I can do?"

"I think the best thing you can do is keep quiet. Let Lord Roland take care of things." Looking about, just to see where we are. Seems to be a cloister: arches on all four sides, and a cobbled square in the middle. "We'll sit down here and wait for him. I don't suppose he'll be long."

There are stone benches set around the cloister garth, most of them speckled with bird droppings. Who's supposed to be cleaning these? Because whoever they are, they're not doing a very good job of it. At Saint Joseph's I'd have been beaten bloody for leaving the benches in this state. It's hard to find a clear spot that's big enough for a single backside.

"Is it true—what Lord Roland said—are you really from Jerusalem?" (Oh, Lord. I should have known. Didn't even give me time to sit down.) "I've never met someone who was born in the Holy Land."

"There are quite a few of us, you know."

"Yes, of course." She sounds faintly apologetic. "You must be tired of people asking questions. But it's hard to imagine what it must be like."

"I suppose so."

"I had a friend, once. She went there on pilgrimage. She said it was wonderful."

"It isn't that wonderful." Sudden memory of the view from the Mount of Olives. Dust and loose gravel under your toes. White roofs in the sunlight. The Golden Gate, the spire of Saint Anne's, the gleaming dome of the Temple. The flocks in the valley. The burning, arching sky. "But it's better than this."

"I'm sorry." Her gentle voice. "Perhaps one day you'll see it again. Perhaps you'll go back."

"Oh, we'll be going back, all right. As soon as the armies of Christendom are raised, we'll be going back to run the Turks out of the kingdom. We're only in Languedoc to find more troops."

"You mean you're doing that now?" She seems concerned. "Raising an army?"

"Well, yes. In a way."

"But are you sure it's the right thing to do?"

The right thing to do? What a bizarre question. "Of course it is. It's a Crusade. Against the Infidels."

"But there will be so much killing. So much blood. Must all those people lose their lives, just for another piece of earth?"

"It's for Jerusalem!"

"Jerusalem is a piece of earth. It's not a piece of heaven."

"Jerusalem is the birthplace of our Lord Jesus

Christ." (Roland's voice. God help us. He nearly scared me to death, sneaking up like that.) "Jerusalem is the Lord's footstool."

"Jerusalem is where Christ came to earth in the shape of a man," Esclaramonde rejoins, craning her neck to look up at him. "But earth is our prison and the realm of the Evil One. Not a single mile of it is worth killing for."

Well, I'll be damned. "Is that what you believe? That the whole world is the work of Satan?" (No wonder she's in trouble.)

"I believe that the world is part of the kingdom of darkness, governed by the Devil, just as heaven is the kingdom of light, governed by God," she replies. "I believe that the world is hell, and that human souls are fragments of the kingdom of light, trapped in earthly bodies that will not rise again at the Last Judgment, because they are part of the kingdom of darkness. And I believe that Jesus Christ, who was not a real man but God's spirit from heaven, showed us how we might free our souls from the earthly prisons they inhabit by living a holy life—"

"Be silent." Roland cuts her off. His tone is harsh, anxious, flustered. "I don't want you talking like this in front of Pagan. You must not talk of these things again, do you understand? Never. Or you must go away at once."

Oh, leave the poor woman alone. She's harmless enough. She just thinks she's a speck of light in a kingdom of darkness. And she certainly hasn't convinced me.

"What happened, my lord?" (Trying to distract him.) "Did you talk to the Abbot? Did you calm him down?"

"Who? Oh, the Abbot." Roland shakes his head. "I'm afraid the Abbot is unconvinced, although I told him about the axe. Tomorrow morning, when he's had time to reflect, I will approach him again. It seems to me that the best thing would be to have one of his monks visit Lavalet, and see Garnier, and talk to Garnier's family."

"You mean they're going to let us stay here? Overnight?" (I don't believe it.)

"There is nowhere else for us to go," he replies. "I pointed this out to the Abbot, when he—when he talked of expelling Mistress Maury. I pointed out that we couldn't, in Christian charity, let her sleep in the forest by herself." His solemn glance shifts to Esclaramonde and back to me again. "You and I are always welcome, the Abbot said, but she must return home as soon as possible, tomorrow morning."

Esclaramonde lifts her chin.

"I will do that willingly," she declares. "I have no wish to stay longer."

Hear, hear. I'm with the lady. This place makes my skin crawl.

‡CHAPTER EIGHT‡

"Ouch!"

"Pagan, will you hold still?"

"Let me do it. I'll do it. You're hurting me."

"No, you're too rough. You'll break the comb. You always break the comb, and this is the only one we have left. I don't want you breaking it."

Tug, tug. He has no idea. Ouch! Knots are plain torture.

"Why do I have to comb it, anyway? Why don't I just cut it all off?"

"With what? Hold still." His hand, pressing my head down. "I wasn't trained to cut hair with a sword. Neither were you. We'll cut it when we get back home. I think my father still has my mother's scissors." (Ouch!) "It ought to be cut. If it gets any longer, you'll have to start plaiting it."

Knock-knock-knock. A gentle tap on the door. Whoops! Get up, Pagan. If anyone sees Roland picking away at your head like that, they'll think he must be delousing you.

"Come in!" Rising to his feet, with the comb still in his hand. Hasn't put his belt on yet.

The door opens slightly.

"My lord Roland?" A monk with a harelip. Seems to be the wrong shape for his robe. "Good morning, my lord. The Abbot wants you."

"The Abbot?"

"If you please."

Roland glances in my direction. "What about my squire?" he says. "And Mistress Maury?"

"He wants all of you, right now."

Hmmm. Wonder what's happened. Roland reaches for his belt. "Pagan, you're dressed. Go and rouse her. We'll be with you in a moment."

"Yes, my lord." Now, where did they put Esclaramonde? In the room next door? That's right. I remember. Turn left, and just a few steps down the passage: *knock-knock-knock.*

"Mistress? It's me, Pagan. You're wanted."

Can't hear anything. Do you think she's awake

yet? Perhaps she's still asleep. Perhaps I ought to knock again.

The door swings open.

Her room's almost identical to ours. Your basic monastic cell, with the usual white walls and polished floor and plain oak chest. There's a candle on the chest and a basin on the floor. One narrow bed instead of two.

But as for Esclaramonde—I can't believe it. Will you look at that hair! As black as jet, thick and glossy, flowing all the way down to her ankles. I've never seen anything so fine.

"What is it?" she says. "Are you ready to leave?"

"Hmm? Oh—yes—I mean no. No. The Abbot wants to see us. What beautiful hair you have."

"Thank you." Stiffly.

"It must be impossible to comb, though. It must take hours. Don't you feel like cutting it off sometimes?"

"Saint Paul said that if a woman has long hair it is a glory to her, for her hair is given for a covering."

Oh, right. I remember that bit. Isn't that where it says: if a man has long hair, it is a shame unto him?

I've really got to get my hair cut.

"Pagan? Ah." It's Roland. He catches sight of Esclaramonde and blinks. (What do you think, my

91

lord? Isn't it beautiful?) Drags his gaze away with what looks like a bit of an effort. "We must hurry," he says.

"But my hair—"

"Leave it."

Yes, leave it. We can't wait around for the rest of the day while you fix up your hair. Anyway, I want to see how the monks react. This one's already speechless. Keeps glancing back over his shoulder as we bustle along the passage. A little more, a little more, and—yes! He almost falls down a flight of stairs turning the first corner.

What a joke.

"This way, my lord," he pants. "This way."

Whoops! And there's another stricken monk. Stops in his tracks to stare after us. What time is it, I wonder. Looks quite early. I think I heard the bell for Terce not long ago. That's one thing you can say about monasteries. As long as you're in one, you've always got a pretty good idea of the time.

"Just through here, please. This way." A lintel set low in a sandstone wall. (Roland has to stoop to pass under it.) And here we are in the cloister garth again. More monks, huddled in groups. A buzz of voices. A servant, dressed for the harvest.

Fresh blood sprinkled on the ground.

"My lord." Tugging the skirt of Roland's surcoat. Pointing out the blood (discreetly). Roland's expression doesn't change: he just nods and keeps walking, across the cobbles to the chapter house. At least, I suppose it's the chapter house. It's certainly where the chapter house should be. Big, bronze doors standing open. Beyond them, a beautiful tiled floor and tiers of wooden seats set under the windows. (Lovely stained glass.) A domed roof, blue, with golden stars painted on it. Monks everywhere . . .

"Aribert!"

Esclaramonde darts forward. Roland catches her, pulling her back. There's a man, moaning, at the other end of the room. He's slumped between two hefty servants, who are dressed in dirty work boots and tunics hitched up to show their bare, scratched knees. Blood drips slowly from his nose, his mouth, his right hand, his temple.

"What have you done?! What have you done to him?" She pulls and squirms, but Roland won't let go. "Aribert! Talk to me! What did they do?"

"You know this man?" It's the Abbot. Sitting to one side, his back hunched, breathing heavily. Any moment now he's going to keel over and expire.

"Of course I know him! It's Aribert! Ow!"

"Be still," says Roland. Speaking in his most ominous tone. She subsides, of course—and so does everyone else. You don't argue with that voice. "What's going on, Lord Abbot?" (Very calm. Very courteous.) "Who is this man, and why is he here?"

"Your friend can tell you that. I cannot. I don't know him."

"It's Aribert! *Aribert!* Garnier's eldest son." Esclaramonde's hands are shaking. "Look what they—how could they do that? How?"

I've got to admit, he looks pretty bad. Nose mashed all over his face. Mouth a bloody hole. Fingers shattered. Somebody's really put the boot in.

"This man has assaulted our servant Clairin," the Abbot reveals. (Cough, cough, cough.) "Clairin was harvesting corn in the southern field, and this man struck him with a scythe. Clairin is now in the infirmary."

"Surely the infirmary is where this man belongs, also," Roland says, in his quiet way. But the Abbot strikes the floor with his staff.

"This man belongs at the end of a rope!" he squawks. "He tried to kill one of my men!"

"Oh, but why?" Esclaramonde groans. "Why, Aribert, why? I've told you again and again. 'Put up thy sword into his place, for those that take the sword shall perish with the sword.'"

No reply from Aribert. I don't think he's even conscious.

"My lord Abbot, this man needs care." Roland's still trying to keep things civilized. "I don't know who did this to him, and I'm not going to ask, but if he's to undertake any traveling—"

"Traveling? Oh, no. He isn't going anywhere."

"My lord, this man is under my father's jurisdiction."

"He is not."

Roland takes a deep breath, and lets it out slowly. "My father," he says, with grinding patience, "has judicial rights over every man, woman, and child at Lavalet. Just as you, my lord, have judicial rights over servants such as Clairin. Now, I know my father is quite satisfied that you should pronounce judgment on Clairin, as long as he is compensated for the wood Clairin has stolen. But you must allow my father the right to pronounce judgment on Aribert, for *his* crime."

The Abbot scowls.

"Clairin is a victim," he says, "not a criminal."

Oh, right. And my auntie Eleanor was the Queen of Persia. What a dung-head.

"Lord Abbot." Roland's beginning to get annoyed. He actually clears his throat. "Lord Abbot, if it hadn't been for Clairin's own actions—"

"There is no proof that Clairin did anything to deserve such an assault!"

"My lord, this was clearly an act of revenge—"

"Nonsense!"

God preserve us. The expression in Roland's eyes! Suddenly he looks just a little bit like Galhard.

"Abbot Tosetus," he says stiffly, "I would appreciate it if you would adopt a respectful tone when you speak to me." (Every word chipped from a block of granite with a blade of Damascus steel.) "There is no need for discourteous behavior."

Gulp. Heads down, everyone. The Abbot mumbles something and coughs. Esclaramonde stares. A handful of monks actually cross themselves.

"My apologies," the Abbot finally remarks, wheezing and gurgling like a water mill. "I am not well, as you can see. You may tell your father, Lord Roland, that I will examine this matter regarding Clairin's alleged trespass. And if any wood was taken, then Lord Galhard will receive it back in full measure."

"Thank you."

"Providing that Lord Galhard also returns the two dozen sheep that his men have stolen from me."

"But—"

"Perhaps, when the sheep have been returned, I will consider restoring this criminal to your father's jurisdiction."

Oh, God. Worse and worse. Glancing at Roland. What's he going to do? Grab the old bog-brain and shake some sense into him?

But no, of course not. If there's one thing that doesn't rule Roland, it's his temper. He simply clenches his teeth, folds his arms, and thinks for a moment. At last he finds his voice again.

"You are an old man and a sick man, and for this reason I can find the heart to forgive your gross ill-breeding and unreasonable prejudice," he announces. "I cannot, however, allow this matter to rest. If the Bishop will not bring his authority to bear, I will go to the lords of Montferrand. I believe they have rights of jurisdiction over this abbey. I also believe that they have a proper understanding of the responsibilities attached to such rights. You, it seems, have forgotten all the understanding you ever possessed."

(That's telling him.)

"Many years ago, I regarded this abbey as a

97

place of truth and virtue and piety," Roland continues. "Now I see that it has been cast down from heaven unto earth, like the daughter of Zion. And I grieve for its desolation."

He straightens his back, turns on his heel, heads for the door. Looks as though we're leaving.

Esclaramonde hesitates.

"Let's go." Touching her arm. Come on, Mistress, before they decide to keep us here after all.

"Yes! Go! Get out!" The Abbot waves his walking stick. It's a pretty feeble gesture. He can hardly lift it off the ground. "Follow that path you have chosen! You are following a writhing serpent down a sink and abyss of errors! The assembly of the wicked have enclosed you, my lord! Beware, for the wicked watcheth the righteous, and seeketh to slay him! *The words of her mouth are smoother than butter, but war is in her heart!*"

"How can you say that?" Esclaramonde cries. "I do not want bloodshed! It's you who are violent! You are the one with war in your heart!"

Oh, hell. "Mistress Maury—"

"Please, Lord Abbot, I beg you." She falls to her knees. Hands outstretched. "Be merciful. Don't shed any more of this man's blood. Be ye therefore merciful, as your Father also is merciful—"

98

Roland! Help! What shall I do? Turning to see where he is—and he's already retracing his steps. "Come," he murmurs. (Dragging her upright.) "Come, there is nothing more we can do here."

"Condemn not, and ye shall not be condemned!" she pleads. "Are we greater than God, we sinners, to pass judgment on other sinners? He that is without sin among you, let him first cast a stone!"

What a terrific preacher she'd make. And she's strong, too. It's quite a task, pulling her toward the doorway.

"Aribert!" she shouts, twisting her head to catch one last glimpse. "Aribert! My prayers are with you! God loves you, Aribert!"

Stumbling into the cloister garth.

"I'll take her to the stables and saddle the horses," Roland says quietly, putting his mouth to my ear. "You get our things. Can you find the stables by yourself?"

"Yes, my lord."

"My lord." Esclaramonde grips his arm with both hands. "My lord, must we leave him? Is there nothing you can do?"

"No, I'm sorry."

"He'll be all right, Mistress." (She's really taking this hard, isn't she?) "I've seen worse, truly. And

99

they were always up and walking within a couple of weeks."

"So much violence," she whispers. "So much blood." Her face is as white as chalk. You'd think she was actually ill, just to look at her.

It's almost frightening.

"If only there was something I could do!" she cries.

"You can pray," says Roland. "There is always prayer. Pagan, if you need help, you should call a monk. And don't dawdle."

No chance of that. Just watch me. I'll stir up such a wind, it'll bring the roof down.

‡CHAPTER NINE‡

Yawn, yawn. What a bore. Nothing to look at. Nothing to eat. Not much of a road, this one. A real goat track, hemmed in by scrubby forest: the occasional oak, lots of sweet chestnuts, wild thyme, campions, and other things I don't recognize. Little brown birds. Twit, twit, twit. Enough to drive you crazy.

No wonder Roland's on edge. He doesn't like riding through forests. Personally, I think he's overreacting a little, because any snot-nosed peasant who attacked Roland would have to have his brain in a splint. He wouldn't last as long as a fish in the Dead Sea.

"There." Esclaramonde points. At last! A break in the trees. More sunlight, and the cleared land unfolds as we draw closer. Trees thin out. The wind picks up. A field of ripe barley. A stone fence. A sickly olive grove. And skulking behind it, a huddle of houses.

Two small dwellings; stables; a winter storehouse. Another building, large and sturdy, which I can't identify. Smoke drifting from a hole in one of the thatched roofs.

"Is this where you live?" Roland asks. He doesn't sound surprised, but I know he is. It's the way his mouth moves. Must have expected something more lavish.

"Yes," Esclaramonde replies. "This is the hospice."

So it's a hospice, is it? I hope it's not for lepers. Moving slowly past the olive trees, toward the muddy ruts of the farmyard. Doesn't seem to be anyone about. Not many animals, either. No chickens. No sheep. No ducks or pigs or dogs. Just the two workhorses, grazing in a paddock by the stables.

"What happened to your livestock?" (I can't help asking.) "Were they stolen?"

"No." She seems distracted. Scans her surroundings for a friendly face. "We don't eat meat. Or eggs."

"But why?" That's crazy. "I don't understand."

"Meat and eggs are born of the flesh by generation or fornication, which is the greatest sin because it condemns another soul to imprisonment on earth," she rejoins. "And besides, it's a sin to kill animals or birds. They too have their holy spirits, which pass from one body to another."

Weird. Glance at Roland, who frowns back ferociously. No religious dialogues, Pagan.

Esclaramonde prepares to dismount.

"Wait." Roland's tone stops her. "Where are your friends?"

"I don't know. Inside, I assume."

"How many live here?"

She thinks for a moment. "Twelve, including me. And Aribert, of course."

"Are they usually inside at this time of day?"

"Well, no. But—"

"Stay there." Roland swings his leg over Fennel's back and slips gracefully to the ground. "Pagan, you'll have to hold the horses. Don't leave this spot unless I summon you."

"Yes, my lord."

"Wait." This time it's Esclaramonde who speaks. "What are you doing? Where are you going?"

"This place is small and unprotected," Roland

responds. "It's vulnerable to attack. I want to check inside. Make sure that everything's safe."

"Of course it's safe. We've never been attacked here. Who would attack us?"

Who would attack you? Stupid woman. Anyone with long fingernails and half a dozen pointed sticks would make a slaughterhouse of this place. Just look at it! You couldn't be more tempting if you had a roast pork supper laid out for visiting brigands.

Roland decides not to argue. He draws his sword as he turns to face the nearest building: a long, low farmhouse with shuttered windows. His blade flashes like silver in the sunlight.

"Stop!" Esclaramonde slides to earth clumsily, making her horse shy. "You can't do that! Put that away! Please! Put that away right now!"

I don't believe it. Put that away? Who does she think she's talking to? Roland stares in astonishment.

"No swords, not here," she gasps, seizing Roland's arm. "You mustn't. It's wrong. You'll frighten them—"

Roland tries to shake her off, but she clings like a limpet.

"Get back," he orders. "Get back! Now!"

"Put your sword away!"

"Let go!"

"Put your sword away!"

"Are you mad?" he exclaims, more surprised than angry. "Where is your reason? I am here to protect you."

"I won't let you go in there with a drawn sword!"

"It's for your own safety, woman!"

"Put up thy sword into his place!"

"Get back on that horse!"

Suddenly someone emerges from the farthest dwelling. A tall, middle-aged woman in a blue robe. She heads straight for Esclaramonde, who drops Roland's arm.

"Garsen!"

"Esclaramonde—"

"What's happened? Where is everyone?"

"Praise God that you're here." Garsen has a face like a watchtower wall, but her voice is surprisingly gentle. "Garnier is dying. His soul must be freed from his body. He needs the blessing of the *consolamentum*, and you're the only one here who can pass on the Holy Spirit."

"But didn't you—?"

"This morning we sent Aribert to Saint-Martin-la-Lande, to bring back a Good Man. But he hasn't returned."

And he won't, either. Esclaramonde glances up at Roland, who says nothing. So she turns back to her friend.

"Garsen, this is—this is Lord Galhard's son Lord Roland Roucy de Bram. And his squire, Pagan."

Garsen drops to one knee. As she rises again, Esclaramonde continues.

"They haven't eaten since last night, and they still have a long way to go. Can you fetch them some food, Sister? Maybe some bread and herbs—there should be almond cakes, too."

"First I will see Garnier," Roland interrupts. "Did you say he was dying?"

"Soon he will surrender his soul," Garsen intones. "May God have mercy."

"Then I will see him. Where is he? Show me the way."

Seems to have forgotten my existence. Wouldn't be the first time, either. "My lord? My lord! What about me? Am I supposed to watch the horses?"

"Yes," he says. But changes his mind. "No, wait. On second thought, I don't want—Mistress, I'd be obliged if you could watch these horses."

"Yes, you stay, Garsen." (Esclaramonde.) "I'll send Othon out, and then you can get the food."

Dismounting, slowly. God preserve us! The soles of my feet are numb. Bones cracking like wood in a fire. Stomach making animal noises.

"Come, Pagan, we haven't got all day."

Oh, go and eat yourself with braised onions. I'm doing the best I can. Crippling my way across the choppy sea of dried mud, with Roland and Esclaramonde walking side by side ahead of me. He's all right, but she's having problems. Sore back, by the look of it. That mount was much too big for her—all the horses in Galhard's stables are built like the Palace of the Patriarchs. She must be exhausted. Passing over a threshold into unrelieved dimness.

"Esclaramonde!" A voice. A room. A cluster of people. Lots of them, all gathered around two feeble, flickering lamps. And a man on a bed . . .

That's got to be Garnier. His head is swathed in grayish bandages. Can't see his eyes. Dried blood in his nostrils and his swollen, purple mouth.

The rattle of his breathing.

Faces turn toward us. Tears glisten in the lamplight, which throws great looming shadows up the unplastered surface of the walls. Beaten earth underfoot. A smell of dampness. Someone's sobbing loudly (Garnier's wife?) and clutching his hand in both of hers.

This is awful. Just awful. I wish I'd stayed with the horses now.

"Oh, Sister. At last." Another woman dressed in blue: young, thin, pale, and about as sturdy as a flake of chaff. "The *consolamentum*, quickly. You must lay your hands on him, before it's too late."

Whispers around the room, but Esclaramonde seems reluctant. She hesitates, biting the end of her thumb. Roland steps forward.

"Is this Garnier?"

A moan from the sobbing woman. She casts herself across the dying man's chest, calling out his name.

"Garnier! Garnier!" Someone rubs her back, helplessly.

"This is Garnier," Esclaramonde confirms, in a low voice.

"And where is the witness?" Roland demands. "Is he present? Where is Estolt?"

The crowd stirs. All eyes focus on a slight, grubby fellow about my age, standing near the head of the bed. He has a runny nose and a fairly successful crop of vegetation on his chin.

"Are you Estolt?" Roland asks. He receives a nod in reply. "Did you see the man who struck your father?"

Another nod.

"Who was it?"

Estolt looks at Esclaramonde, who says, "This is Lord Roland of Bram. He's here to help us." (Why do they all seem so frightened?) Estolt wriggles uncomfortably.

"It was Clairin of Saint Jerome," he finally reveals. You can hardly understand what he's saying, his accent's so thick. "Clairin hit my father."

"Do you swear to that? On the blood of Christ?"

"We believe that Christ shed no blood," Esclaramonde breaks in, "because he did not have true human flesh. Also, we do not believe in oaths. Christ said: 'Swear not at all—'"

Suddenly, Garnier's harsh breathing stops. Someone screams. *"Father! Father!"* Bodies press forward.

Esclaramonde is shoved toward the bed.

"Hurry, Sister, hurry! Give him the holy spirit!"

Ouch! Get off my foot! It's hard to see, but there's Garnier's nose. And there's Esclaramonde's hand, two hands, hovering just above the dying man's forehead. Her voice is shaky, but firms up as she gets into her stride.

". . . and the Word was with God, and the Word was God. . . . All things were made by Him, and without Him was not anything made that was made. In Him was life, and the life was the light of men. And the light shineth in darkness, and the darkness comprehended it not. . . ."

"Pagan." A hand on my elbow. What? What's up? "Come here, quickly." Roland fishes me out of the throng the way you'd fish a bit of garlic sausage out of a cassoulet. Dragging me out the door and into the sunshine. Clean, sweet air.

"What is it, my lord?" He looks sick. Was it the stuffy atmosphere? "Are you all right?"

"Yes, yes. But I should have stopped it."

"Stopped what?"

"In there — that — that blasphemy."

"What blasphemy?"

"What they were doing. I don't know what it was. But there was no priest — no holy water —"

"My lord, that was the Gospel of Saint John. I swear. They used to read it out all the time at Saint Joseph's."

He blinks. "Are you sure?"

"Of course I'm sure. You know me. Memory like the Book of Life."

He looks back, undecided. A wary, watchful expression on his face. Scratching his left shoulder with his right hand.

Garsen's still waiting with the horses.

"My lord." (Come on, Roland. Get a grip on yourself.) "They have no priest or holy water here. They're doing the best they can. Can't we just let them be, and eat something? We'll have to be going soon, remember."

There. That's done it. He nods and walks across to where Garsen is standing. Takes the reins from her hand. "Tell me," he says, "who is Esclaramonde? Where does she come from?"

"Esclaramonde is a Good Woman," Garsen replies softly. "Her husband was a citizen of Carcassonne. He was killed by brigands, and her baby son died soon after, from a terrible illness. In her grief, she turned away from the false church of Rome and became a member of the church of Good Men. She came here to live in peace. To pray. To live a holy life, close to God."

"And you? And the others? Why are you here?"

"My lord, we too wish to lead holy lives. Also, we had nowhere else to go."

She trots off to fetch us some edibles, leaving

Roland lost in thought. He always takes everything so seriously. Why bother yourself about a bunch of heretics? They're no threat. They don't even like fighting. It's the Infidels we have to worry about.

Anyway, it seems to me that Esclaramonde is a very pious woman. More pious than most of the other people I've met. It's just that she's got some peculiar ideas.

"Lord Roland?" Speak of the Devil. There she is, Esclaramonde, emerging from the shadowy doorway. Seems quite calm, although she moves as if her joints are stiff. Face white and grim above her black robe.

Roland steps forward to meet her.

"My lord, I want to apologize for raising my voice," she says. "'He that is slow to anger is better than the mighty.' I ask your forgiveness."

It's like talking to a slab of granite. Roland's frozen up again.

"There is nothing to forgive," he replies brusquely.

"And please — please — is there any way of stopping what has begun here?" She looks up at him, her voice solemn. "Garnier is dead. The man who killed him is badly wounded. Aribert is . . .

Aribert may be lost to us. I don't believe that any good will come of pursuing this tragedy. It will simply mean more killing. Can you go away and forget it, my lord? Can you forget that it ever happened?"

Roland hesitates.

"It concerns a trespass on my father's lands," he says slowly. "I don't believe that my father can ignore it. Besides, I noticed—I couldn't help noticing that you hardly have any men here. Just women. Now that Garnier is gone, and Aribert, too, how will you manage with only a couple of boys? Surely you must want some compensation?"

"Not at the price of another life!" Esclaramonde protests, and suddenly bursts into tears.

Oh, Lord. Poor thing. Weeping like a waterfall. No help from Roland, of course: he's completely paralyzed. Looks at me in desperation.

Kidrouk to the rescue.

"There, there." A careful arm around her shoulders. (They feel so small.) "It's hard, I know. It's very hard."

"I'm sorry," she sobs. "I can't—can't h-help it."

"Shhh."

"Garnier—so good—"

"He's with Jesus now."

"Yes I know, but . . . the suffering . . . his family . . . and I have to tell them about Aribert. . . ."

Garsen. Thank God. She hurries over to us, a basket in one hand and a jug in the other. Food! At last! (Here, I'll take that.)

"Sister! What's wrong?"

"He's dead, Garsen. He's dead."

"God have mercy. . . ." The two women embrace, as Roland crosses himself. Mmmm. Almond cakes. Will it look terrible if I start eating? After all, I didn't actually know the man.

"Pagan." A gesture from Roland. He speaks very quietly. "We should go now. We can eat on the way. I want to reach Bram before dark."

Hear, hear. No night rides, please. This food can go in a saddlebag. "Have a drink, my lord."

"My lord!" Esclaramonde throws out a hand, and it's wet with tears. "Thank you, my lord. Thank you for your kindness." Poor woman. Poor thing. Look at her sad, grubby little face and her poor, red nose. It's enough to break your heart.

But Roland doesn't respond. He doesn't even smile. He turns away abruptly and puts his foot in a stirrup.

Honestly. I ask you. What's wrong with the man?

✠CHAPTER TEN✠

Noises from the hall. Frantic, rowdy noises. Yells and thumps and bursts of laughter.

I don't know if I can face this.

"Pagan? What's wrong?" Roland, up ahead of me. Peering back through the dusk to where the pathetic remnants of his former squire are hauling themselves, bit by bit, up the outer staircase.

"Oh, my lord . . . I'm so tired. I just want to go to bed."

"You should eat something first."

"No, I can't. Not unless it picks itself up and marches down my gullet." I'm practically asleep now. Going to sleep with my eyes open, like a lion. And Roland doesn't look too fresh himself.

Sweaty. Sunburned. Covered in dust. His white tunic all stained and faded and darned where the saddle's rubbed holes in the linen.

That's what I hate about white. No matter how hard you scrub, you can't get the blood out.

"Well, it's been a long day. And a hard ride." He pats my shoulder. "You can go straight through to bed. I'll just have a word with Lord Galhard about the Abbot."

"Thank you, my lord."

And in we go.

Wham! What a din! Like being hit over the head with a percussion instrument. The whole place is full. Fire blazing. Candles everywhere. Tables pushed back against the walls. Pons kneeling on the dank rushes, blindfolded, his arms outstretched.

Oh, I see. They're playing Hot Cockles.

Ademar darts forward, tapping Pons lightly on the cheek. He jumps back as Pons lunges. "Germain!" says Pons. Everyone roars with laughter. Hoots and comments from every side.

"Guess again!"

"Close!"

"It was Ademar!"

Now it's Berengar's turn. Walks over and *whoomp!* God preserve us. A blow to the neck that sends

Pons sprawling. I haven't seen the game played like this before.

"L-lord Galhard," Pons gasps, dazed and winded.

"Wrong!"

"Next!"

"Can't you recognize Berengar's right fist? You've had it in your eye often enough!"

Well, I'm not about to hang around here and watch them beat poor Pons to a bloody pulp. Call this Hot Cockles? It looks more like the Battle of Hattin.

I'm going to bed.

Glance at Roland, who nods. Off you go, Pagan. Pushing through the crowds on the perimeter (Aimery, Foucaud, Germain), kicking a path through the dogs, grabbing one of the candles. It's dark on the stairs. Taking things slowly, like a cripple. One step. Two steps. Three steps. At this rate it'll be morning before I reach the top. . . .

Wait. What's that noise? Someone coming up the stairs behind me. God, I hope it's not Isarn. Taking the rest of them two at a time. Hurrying through Berengar's room (which looks like the inside of a goat's stomach—doesn't Isarn ever scrape the spit off the walls?) and into ours. Dropping the saddlebags with a careless clunk.

117

I hate this room. It looks so desolate, especially in candlelight.

"Welcome home, Pagan."

Whirl around, heart thumping.

It's Jordan.

"Oh, hello, my lord." He's leaning against the doorjamb, and he doesn't have his falcon with him. Hair in a tangle. Soiled tunic. Ever so slightly unbalanced around the knees.

Drunk, of course. Absolutely marinated.

"How was your trip?" he murmurs. His drawl is more pronounced. "Was it successful?"

"Lord Roland would be the one to ask about that, my lord."

"I don't want to ask Roland. He's a couple of psalms short of a psalter. I'm asking you."

"Well . . ." Take it gently, Pagan. Don't excite anyone. "It wasn't very successful, as a matter of fact. Mostly because the Abbot of Saint Jerome seems to be suffering from a chronic absence of brain."

Jordan grins fiendishly. He has tiny, pointed teeth like a kitten's.

"How perceptive you are," he drawls. "It's quite true. The Abbot has no brain to speak of. What is it about the clergy, I wonder, that makes them so deficient in this respect? Does the church remove their wits when it gives them a tonsure? Or are brainless people naturally attracted to the church? Witness Roland, for example. Roland enjoys the company of priests, and you wouldn't say that he was exactly overendowed in the upper story, would you?"

"My lord—"

"Oh, don't misunderstand me. Don't misunderstand me, Pagan." He lurches forward, and stands there swaying slightly from foot to foot. "He's a good fighter, good Christian, chivalrous opponent, even a fair-to-middling singer, did you know? But I'd hardly call him a great mind."

"My lord." (I know you're soaked, but that's no excuse.) "My lord, if you think you're amusing me with talk like this, then you're mistaken."

"Is that so?" Softly.

"Lord Roland is my lord. I serve him. I honor him. And I obey him. I also happen to think that he's the noblest man I've ever met. So if you continue to talk this way, I'll—I'll—"

"Yes?" Thrusting his face close to mine. Whew! Wine on the breath. "Please tell me, Pagan. What will you do?"

Good question. "I don't know."

He laughs.

"There's not much I can do, my lord. Except remove myself from your company."

"No, no," he protests. "No, don't do that. You're the only vaguely interesting person who's turned up here in years. Years and years and years. Do you see what I have to put up with every night?" He waves his hand in the general direction of nowhere in particular. "Hot Cockles. Earwig races. Cock fights. They occasionally entertain themselves by chopping the heads off chickens and watching the headless corpses run around our hall."

Well, it doesn't surprise me. "Sounds like fun. When do they do that, on the Feast of John the Baptist?"

"Sometimes I think I'm going to die of boredom." He staggers over to Roland's palliasse and nudges it with the toe of his boot. "Is this where he's sleeping? Not very luxurious, is it? But I suppose Roland's a good campaigner. A good Templar knight. No wine, women, or comfortable beds."

"My lord—"

"You know, Pagan, I think you deserve better than this. So do I, in fact. Comes of being a second son." He mumbles something into his beard. "Stuck in this Godforsaken hole . . ."

"Why don't you get out, then?"

He looks up, his eyes red-rimmed and puffy. "Get out?"

"Like Lord Roland." I wonder if I should have started this. He's peering at me in a rather disturbing way. "Why don't you join the Crusade, my lord? I can guarantee it won't be boring."

"Join the Crusade?" He begins to laugh. "Join the *Crusade*?"

I don't see what's so funny. Other men have. "Of course, if you don't even want to see the world—if you want to molder away in Languedoc—"

"Pagan, Pagan, Pagan." He comes up and puts his hands on my shoulders. (I wish he wouldn't breathe in my face like that!) "How could I possibly let these lands out of my sight? Even for a moment? You never know what may occur."

Hmmm. That's interesting.

"Besides," he continues, "look at Roland. He went away, and now he's back. With what? What has he gained from all those years out there? I'll tell you. He's gained nothing."

"That's not true." Trying to disengage myself from his slightly painful grip. "You just don't understand what he's been looking for. If you want my opinion, he's got a lot more than you have."

"I know. You're right. Because he's got you."

All of a sudden, Roland's voice. "What's going on here?" He's standing on the threshold, a lamp in his hand. "Pagan? What are you doing? I thought you were going to bed."

"Ah! Roland. Speak of the Devil. Or should I say angel?" Jordan pushes himself upright, and almost throws me on my back. Obviously doesn't know his own strength, when he's been drinking. "We were just talking about you, baby brother. Talking about your vices and virtues. I think we decided that you were a man of great courage, and honor, and nobility, but perhaps not all that bright."

"My lord—"

"Quiet, Pagan. I'm talking to your master. You see, Roland, this little gem of a squire—this price-less jewel of gold in a swine's snout—has offered to read me a book. He's going to read me one of Eleanor's books. The one I managed to save during that particularly bad winter when we were burning everything that didn't kick and scream when we picked it up—"

"You have her books?"

"Her book. A single book. Oh, yes, and I'm keeping it. You may have been her favorite, but I've

122

kept her book." Jordan throws one long arm around Roland's shoulders. "So you see, I was just asking this delightful squire of yours if he would deliver me from the tedium of Hot Cockles with a few words of comfort from Eleanor's library—"

Roland suddenly pushes Jordan away, his face tight with suppressed emotion. Anger? Disgust? Shame?

"You're drunk," he says. And Jordan laughs.

"Brilliant! Well spotted! Perhaps you're not so stupid after all."

"Pagan is tired. He's had a long day. He can't read to you now."

"Oh. Well." (Jordan sways alarmingly.) "Perhaps some other time."

"Perhaps," says Roland, "perhaps not. We may be leaving soon."

"Oh no, what a pity. And we were enjoying your company so much."

"Why don't you go to bed, Jordan? Your wife must be wondering where you are."

"My wife?" Jordan spits. "My wife would be quite happy to see me at the bottom of the Garonne, as you well know." He pokes Roland in the chest with one finger. "That's something else you've managed to avoid, isn't it? Among other things. Connubial bliss."

"Good night, Jordan."

"My dear little brother. Always so courteous. And a very good night to you, Piglet." Glancing at me. "We always called him Piglet when he was small. I don't know why. Perhaps because he was so fat—"

"Good *night*, Jordan."

"Good night, Roland. Good night, Pagan. Pleasant dreams."

And off he lurches. Disappearing into his room. Roland lets out a small sigh, and drops his saddlebag. *Clunk!*

"My lord, I swear to you, I didn't say any of those things. Truly . . ."

"I know you didn't. Because I know my brother. My brother is a liar." He collapses onto his palliasse, rubbing his eyes wearily. "That's why I want you to stay away from him. He is not fit company for you."

"Oh, well." (I wouldn't go that far.) "He's all right. He was just a bit drunk—"

"Pagan, did you hear what I said? I said he's a liar. He can't be trusted. He's dangerous." Thrusting his foot at me. (Boots, Pagan.) "I don't want you talking to any of my family, unless it's unavoidable. They are all better left alone, especially Jordan. He is the worst."

"My lord, he can't be as bad as Lord Berengar." Yanking at the supple calfskin boots. "I mean—I don't mean to be rude, my lord, but Lord Jordan seems pretty intelligent—"

"That's why he's more dangerous. I can't—" A pause. "Please, Pagan. Do you think I don't know my own brother? When he was a child, he had a falcon. A little hawk, smaller than the one he has now. My father gave it to him. It was headstrong, and sometimes it wouldn't return when it was called. So Jordan put its eyes out with a burning stick. He said that it would never stray again." Another pause. "It didn't, either. It died. Well, what would you expect? My father was very angry. He set the dogs on Jordan."

"The *dogs*?"

"You can't see Jordan's scars, because he keeps them well covered. He's always been very patient with his hawks, since then."

Jesus. I'll bet he has.

"What I'm trying to tell you, Pagan, is that Jordan has always had the heart of a wolf. Always. He hasn't changed, and he never will. Underneath all this fine talk, he's just a wild beast."

And he's not the only one. What a family! Roland must be some kind of miracle. Either that or a changeling.

He begins to struggle out of his surcoat, dragging it over his head.

"My lord? What did Lord Galhard say about the Abbot?"

"Oh. The Abbot. Yes." His voice is muffled by the folds of white linen. "I offered to take the matter to the Bishop, or to the lords of Montferrand. They have traditional rights of jurisdiction over Saint Jerome, because it was built on their lands. I believe the Abbey was founded by one of their ancestors. Unfortunately . . ." (His tousled head emerges.) "Unfortunately, the Montferrands are not on good terms with my father. And they are vassals of Toulouse, which means that they're in Quercy at the moment, defending the Count's lands against Richard of England."

"So what did Lord Galhard say?"

"That he'd take care of it himself."

Hmmm. Sounds a bit ominous. Glance at Roland, who's frowning down at the crumpled surcoat in his lap. (Needs a good wash, that surcoat.)

"Did he say anything else?"

"He invited us on a hunt tomorrow. Apparently

126

Isarn's found a ten-tine hart. They've been tracking it all day."

A hunt! I've never been on a hunt. But I don't suppose I'll get the chance now.

"Are we going, my lord?"

"Well, normally I wouldn't, because the Rule of the Order discourages it." (Hah! There, what did I tell you?) "But I'm beginning to think we should." He looks up at me with tired, bloodshot eyes. "Just to make sure that it *is* a hunt. We don't want it turning into some kind of raid."

Good point. I'm sure that when Galhard says he'll "take care" of things, it's worth keeping an eye on his movements.

"But you mustn't worry, Pagan, please. Just go to bed, and I'll undress myself." He manages to produce a rather battered smile. "We'll have to rise early in the morning. Hunts always start before dawn around here."

Before dawn! God preserve us.

Maybe I'm not so keen to go hunting after all.

‡CHAPTER ELEVEN‡

"Roland! Oh Ro-o-oland! Wake up, Roland!"

Wha—? Who—? What's happening? What's that? God! Smoke! I can hardly—

"It's time to get u-u-up."

Somebody's voice . . . Berengar's . . . with a torch . . . and Roland's bed! It's burning!

"My lord! Get up!"

Is that him? Hard to see . . .

"My lord!" (Grabbing a blanket.) "My lord!"

Yes, that's him. Through the smoke—on his feet—staggering about. Flames licking the edge of his palliasse.

Berengar, coughing and laughing in one corner.

"Pagan—" Roland can hardly breathe to speak. "Pagan, are you all right?"

"My bed! Get my bed!" Throwing my blanket onto the fire. Stamping on it. (Ouch!) "Drag it over! Hurry!"

Clouds of smoke. Stinging eyes. Flecks of smoldering straw, whirling about. Watch it, Pagan. Watch your hair. . . .

Turn around. Where's Roland? He's got my palliasse. Rush to help him. One—two—three— *heave!*

Casting it onto the embers. *Whump.* Smothering them. If that doesn't put it out, nothing will.

"Water," Roland gasps, "we need water."

"Oh, leave it," says Berengar. "It'll be fine."

"That floor's made of wood!"

"Then I'll piss on it for you."

Wait. Wait a moment. What's Berengar doing with—? That pus-head!

"You tried to kill Roland!" (You wolf. You devil!) "You tried to kill him!"

"Don't be a fool." Berengar sounds drunk. "I tried to wake him up, that's all."

"You set fire to his bed!"

"Lord Galhard told me to wake him up. So I woke him up."

"Pagan." Roland puts a hand on my shoulder. "Be still."

"If I'd wanted to kill him, boy, he wouldn't be standing there now," Berengar continues in slurred tones. "When I kill someone, I do it properly. And you'd better remember that."

Maggot-bag. Crater-face. You're going to pay for this, you unspeakable lump of undigested offal.

"Pagan, please, we have to get out of here." (Roland, tugging at my arm.) "There's too much smoke . . . we need water. . . ."

"No, no, the water can wait," Berengar interrupts. "The old man wants you down in the cellars. It's urgent. Come on." Wheezing and choking, he stumbles back into his room. Foucaud's there. He looks dazed and disheveled and sleepy, forced out of bed by the commotion. Blinking in the torchlight.

"Foucaud," says Roland, coughing fiercely. "There's been—there's been an accident. A fire. Lord Galhard wants me, so I can't finish putting it out. Will you fetch water, and douse the embers in my room? Make sure the floor is soaked. Take the beds outside."

"Come on, Roland!" Berengar clamors. He's already on the stairs.

"Take care of it, Foucaud." Roland moves toward Berengar's bed, with its mantle of furs and dogs and old horse blankets. He pulls a dirty riding cloak out of the mess and tosses it at me. "Wrap yourself in this, Pagan."

Of course. That's right. I've got nothing on my top half. Or on my feet.

Neither does Roland.

"Come on!" Berengar's voice, echoing up the stairwell. Roland digs around a little more, ignoring the whimpering dogs, and produces a tunic so old and frayed and disgusting that it looks as if some bitch has given birth to a litter of puppies on it. Pulling it over his head.

Oh, no, he can't wear that. "My lord, you can't wear that—"

"Come on, Pagan, don't dawdle."

And down the stairs we go. Down, down, down. Treading carefully (it's so dark, and this cloak is so long), past the first floor landing, way down to the cellars. Damper and damper. Colder and colder. What time is it? No light from the windows. A film of water on the stone walls, glistening in the light from Berengar's torch. Slimy puddles on the flag-stones. (I wish I was wearing my boots.) Roland ahead of me, nursing his arm. Why's he—? "My lord! Are you burned?"

"Just a little."

"Where? Let me see!"

"It's nothing. It's a scorch. Don't concern yourself."

Don't concern myself! I swear, I'm going to kill that Berengar. I'm going to stick a lance in his ear and skewer his brains.

"What's that noise?" Roland stops in his tracks, listening. What noise? Oh. That noise.

A faint, muffled cry. And a thump, like somebody pounding on wood.

"Here, I'll show you. This way," Berengar responds. "They're in the granary."

Pushing on, through puddles and cobwebs, through cavernous, half-glimpsed rooms full of sacks and barrels. The squeak and scamper of rats. The sudden, overpowering smell of wine, as rich as plum syrup. The hollow sound of voices, growing louder and louder. And there's another light, praise God. Through the far door, into a long room lined from floor to ceiling with giant wooden vats.

Grain vats? Probably. The floor's gritty with corn and chaff and mouse droppings.

"Roland." It's Galhard. Fully dressed and armed, his face the color of raw beef. Isarn beside him. Joris. Pons. Jordan, looking even more slovenly

132

than he did this evening. "Roland, come and listen to this rat in the grain bin."

What's that funny scratching? Scrapes and thumps and whimpers—there's something inside that vat.

No, not something. Somebody.

"What—what have you done?" Roland exclaims. And everyone else bursts out laughing.

"Big bastard, isn't he?" Berengar crows. "Must have eaten the whole binful."

Roland turns to Galhard. "What have you done, my lord?"

"I told you I'd take care of that Abbot," his father replies smugly. "In my own way."

"This is the *Abbot*?!"

"Hell, no. I wish it was." Galhard thumps the vat with a clenched fist. "This is one of the Abbot's men. What's his name?"

"Guibert," says Jordan.

"Brother Guibert. That's it. Germain informed me that Brother Guibert was staying in the village with our beloved Father Puy, on his way back from Carcassonne. Just passing through. Lucky, wasn't it?"

"You should have seen his face when we burst in!" Berengar adds. "Must have thought the Devil was coming to get him!"

Another moan from inside the vat. Roland appears to be speechless. Shock, I suppose.

"We didn't know where to put him, because the guardroom's full and we've been storing sides of pork in the lockup," Galhard continues. "Then Jordan suggested this brilliant idea. Plenty of room and no way out. Unless we knock that bolt out of the supply door."

"My lord, please, you can't do this." Roland's trying to stay calm, but you can tell he's having trouble. "This won't solve anything."

"Rubbish!" Galhard barks. "The Abbot's got one of my men. Now I've got one of his. If he releases mine, I'll return the favor."

"My lord, this man is an innocent monk—"

"Oh, grow up, Roland." (Berengar.) "You're not in Jerusalem. There are no innocent monks around here."

"My lord—"

"I've made up my mind, Roland." Galhard's voice is more threatening than a drawn sword: it's enough to freeze the hair on your neck. But all at once the captive starts shouting. He pleads for help. He calls to God. His fingernails scrape on wood like a dog's claws.

I've never heard anything so frightful.

"At least let him out of there!" Roland's turned quite pale. "You can't keep him in a grain vat. He's not a field mouse."

"I'll do what I damn well like."

"But he can't even see! And it must be so cold and airless—"

"You're breaking my heart, Roland."

"If it's the cold that worries you, then I suggest you do something about your squire," Jordan remarks. "He's shaking like a leaf, in case you haven't noticed."

Who, me? Suddenly realizing how cold I am. Feet frozen. Teeth chattering. Roland looks around.

"I'll just take him upstairs, shall I?" Jordan offers. But Roland turns on him. "You leave Pagan alone!" Sharply. "He can find his own way."

Of course I can. What am I, a moron? Silently, Jordan passes me his lamp. His hands feel sticky. "Thank you, my lord." (The sooner I get out of here, the better.)

"My lord, there must be some other option." Stubbornly Roland resumes his attack. "I'm sure that a single guard would be just as secure as this arrangement. . . ." His voice fades as I move out of earshot, into the darkness. Splashing through puddles, looking for the stairs. I remember those barrels — and that milk churn — and the thing that looks like a coffin. It's a sharp left here, isn't it? Left and then right. Under this archway. Along this corridor . . . and at last they appear. The stairs. Hallelujah!

Praise the Lord, who brought me out of an horrible pit. There's no way I'm going down there again.

Thump! Thump! Thump! A funny sound above my head, like someone dragging a body down a flight of steps. Getting closer as I clear the first landing. *Thump! Thump! Thump!* Oh, no. It's not a body. It's Foucaud, dragging Roland's wet palliasse. The smell of scorched hemp is enough to make your eyes water.

"Where are you taking that, Foucaud?"

"Lord Roland told me to take it outside."

"Oh, yes." (I remember now.) "But where are we going to sleep?"

He just goggles at me like a dead fish. What a bonehead. "Never mind." Stumbling past him, up the stairs to Berengar's room. More smoke, more smells. Pushing past a couple of dogs, and through the door to our luxurious chamber. The floor is soaking wet. Oh, for God's sake! That stupid, snot-faced, oyster-eyed idiot! He's damn well soaked our saddlebags, as well!

"Foucaud, you fool! Oh, you festering fool!"

Pulling out my clothes—they're all sodden. My palliasse dripping. My blanket a pool of mush. "God damn it! God damn you!" Kicking at the wet firewood. "God damn all of you! I hate this place!"

"Pagan?" Roland's voice, from Berengar's room. "What's wrong?"

"Oh, my lord . . ."

"What?" He appears in the doorway, his face smeared with soot and ash. He looks as if he's been dragged through a field of nettles.

"My lord, look what they've done! Everything's wet through!"

"It doesn't matter. We'll borrow something."

"They must have boiled tripe for brains!"

"Please, Pagan, please." He puts his hand to his head. I've never seen him make a gesture like that before. "Don't shout."

Don't shout? I wasn't shouting. What's the matter with him?

"Are you all right, my lord?"

"No. Yes. Of course." Standing there, with his eyes closed, and his hand on his forehead. "Just be quiet for a moment, please."

Fine. Sure. I'll be quiet. Not another word will pass my lips. Wringing out my tunic—and my cloak. My stockings look like dead eels. Even my boots are full of water.

Suppose we'll have to sleep in the chapel until this floor's dry. Not that we'll be getting any more sleep tonight, I'll bet. The instant we lie down we'll probably have to get up again, if hunting starts as early as he said it would.

"Pagan."

Who, me? Surely not. You don't want to talk to me. I'm the quiet one, remember?

"Pagan, I know this is hard. But I just can't leave. Not yet."

Looking up at him. Leave? Who said anything about leaving?

"Something bad is going to happen. I know the signs. It's always like this, every spring." He smoothes back his hair. "A kind of madness. I can't go away and let it escalate. How can I? I'm a Templar. I have a duty to keep the peace."

Keep the peace! Hah! You'll be lucky to keep your sanity in this dump.

"Do you understand, Pagan?"

"Of course I understand. I'm not stupid." That's why I can see that you're ramming your head against a stone wall. These people don't even want your help, Roland. You should go away and let them hack each other to pieces.

Otherwise, they're going to drag you down with them.

‡CHAPTER TWELVE‡

How terrible to think that for all these years, I've missed out on the joys of hunting. The thrill of standing behind a bush for half a day. The breathless excitement of gnat bites. The gut-wrenching sound of dogs sniffing each other's genitals. Now I can see what all the fuss is about.

"Raven! Sit!" You stupid hound. Trying to untangle leashes as the three of them weave in and out, panting and sniffing, occasionally growling, occasionally lifting their legs. By God, they're strong, though. My hands are getting tired. I'm just not cut out to be a dog varlet.

This hunting horn, for instance. I've never even blown one before. What happens if I can't manage it? What if I can't make any noise? Will it matter if I just release the dogs without a signal? Surely not. Maybe I can shout or something. That would warn the hunting party that my reinforcements have been unleashed.

"Yours will be three of the slower, steadier hounds." Isarn's voice suddenly fills my head. *"They'll add speed when the main pack is flagging, and they're not as hard to control as the younger dogs. Just wait until the others have passed before releasing them. That's all you have to do."*

Yes, but how am I going to know when the others have passed? You didn't even tell me how many dogs there would be in the main pack. Ten? Twelve? Supposing they come in small groups? Supposing they don't come at all?

If they don't come soon, I'm going to die of boredom. Either that, or these dogs will eat me. They seem to be getting pretty desperate. Haven't eaten anything but bread and dripping since their last hunt, according to Berengar. "Never feed meat to your hunting dogs" is his motto. "Meat is only for the kill."

Yes, but what kill? I don't like the way Beelzebub is eyeing my ankle.

Suddenly Raven lifts his head. The other dogs stiffen. They bare their teeth, and a growl ripples Samson's throat.

Is it them? Is it the pack?

Peering through the undergrowth, through the light and shade. Can't see anything. Can't hear anything, either. Oh, wait. Yes, I can. Was that the sound of barking?

Woof!

"Shut up, Samson!" How can I hear with all that noise going on? Waiting and waiting. The smell of hot dog. The smell of crushed leaves. Flapping away at a cloud of gnats, my heart pounding in my ears. There! No. Yes! A rustle—sticks breaking—something heavy crashes through the brush nearby.

Woof! Woof-woof-woof! The dogs give tongue. They strain at their leashes and gnash their fangs. "Raven! Samson! Sit!" Another dog answers, from somewhere to the south. God! It's them. And that noise—it must have been the stag. It must have passed us!

Fumbling for my horn with one hand, trying to hold those damned dogs with the other. They're going to choke themselves if they carry on like that. "Samson! Sit!" My mouth is so dry. Can you blow a horn with a dry mouth?

Suddenly a dog leaps into sight. Heavily jowled, large ears: a typical lymer hound. And another. Their tongues flapping like pink flags. And there's a man, too, but I can't make out who it is. He's moving too fast. Someone in blue? He disappears again, as more dogs shuffle through the grass, panting and sniffing.

"Samson!" Too late. He's jerked out of my grip and plunged after the others. Oh, well, I suppose he knows the game better than I do. Just hope he doesn't catch that leash on something and strangle himself.

Time to release the other two.

Bending down to let them loose. They disappear before I have time to draw breath. Quick! The horn! Lips on the thin end. Fill your lungs and:

Paaarp!

I did it! I did it! Praise ye the Lord, praise Him with the sound of trumpets! Suddenly, from far away, a chorus of other horns. What—? Who—? Wait a moment. . . .

They can't have got that far.

Shouts from someone close by. Can't make out what he's saying. Perhaps I should join him? Moving forward, dodging a low branch, stumbling on a tangle of roots. I'm not used to forest like this. It's so thick and misleading.

"You!" Isoard bursts out of a thicket. "Did you blow that horn?"

"Which horn?"

"It was you, wasn't it? Damn your eyes!" His hair is plastered with sweat. His clothes are torn, and his chest is heaving. "You butter-brain! You fool! Can't you tell the difference between an alaunt and a lymer hound?"

"Of course I can—"

"Then why did you unleash? We're with Isarn and the lymers! We're driving the damn thing! The hunting party's down there, waiting!"

Uh-oh. He grabs my sleeve, and we push our way through a clump of hawthorn. The ground's very rough underfoot. Ouch! That hurt.

"I can't believe it." (Muttering to himself.) "There were only five hounds. No horses. I can't believe it."

Dogs, frantically barking. Voices raised. Staggering into a cleared patch, carpeted with thyme. Isarn's there, waving his arms at somebody dressed in red, who shoots up the nearest slope, whistling. The dogs mill around in widening circles.

"Isarn!" Isoard cries, and Isarn turns.

Gulp.

"So it was you! You stupid little tick!"

Oh, God. "I'm sorry, Isarn—"

144

Oof! A blow across the ear.

"Are you blind, you castrate? Didn't you see me? I'm the huntsman, God curse you!"

Crack! Stars. Lurching. My knees give way.

"Do you see what you've done, you miserable Turk?! Your alaunts have outrun my lymers and chased the hart off to the east! To the east! The cover's as thick as a ram's fleece over there!" (Grabbing my hair. Ow! Ouch!) "Alaunts aren't trackers! They'll have lost it for sure!"

"Let go—"

"Let go! If we've lost that hart, you dung-worm, I'll send those dogs after *you!*"

"Isarn." It's Isoard's voice. And what's that? Something else. A horn. More dogs. More voices.

Suddenly the clearing's filled with people on horseback. Lots of stamping and snorting and tossing heads. Berengar wants to know what's going on. One of the dogs comes up and sniffs at the blood on my hand.

Where's that from? My nose? No, my lip.

"It wasn't my horn. It was his horn. We weren't ready." (Isarn, explaining that it was all my fault.) "We were driving it south, toward you, but the alaunts pushed it east. I sent someone after them . . . should be able to catch up . . ."

"You mean we'll have to start again?" Berengar's booming protest.

"Oh, no, the hart can't have gone too far. It's nervous, but it's not running hard yet. The slots on the tracks are too close together."

"Get going, then," Galhard exclaims. "Hurry."

Better stand up, I suppose. (If I can.) Scratched knees. Throbbing ear. Four dusty black legs appear in front of me. Raise my eyes, and it's Roland. Mounted on Galhard's spare hunting hack.

"Is this true, Pagan?" He doesn't look very happy. "Did you let those hounds off the leash?"

"My lord—" (Don't *you* start! It wasn't my fault! I didn't know!) "I thought—I thought—"

"Weren't you listening? I explained it to you at least three times."

"That Turk's not handling any more dogs," Galhard declares. "He's out of the hunt. Get rid of him."

"Here." (Joris.) "Let me."

"No, let me." It's Berengar. "I'll tie him by the ankle and drag him the rest of the way!"

"That's far too good for him. I vote we let the dogs loose."

God preserve us. I'm dead. They'll kill me, and I've ruined everything. Trying to stand still. Trying to blink the tears away. Blood all over my hands. "I'm sorry. I'm so sorry."

Someone spits, and it's deadly accurate. Lands on my forehead.

"Dirty Turk."

"Infidel."

"That's enough!" Roland, crisply. "Leave him alone."

"Good idea," Aimery says. "Let's leave him alone. He can find his own way back to the castle."

"No he can't. Come here, Pagan." Roland reaches down and extends a hand. "You can sit up behind me, out of harm's way."

"You're not bringing him along?!" Berengar cries.

"I'm not sending him back on foot."

"But you'll never keep up!"

"I will if the hart's running tired. He won't be any trouble: I'll make sure he's well out of the way. Come on, Pagan, hurry."

How can you talk like that? How can you sit there and look so—so—can't you see what I'm feeling?

"Come on, Pagan." He puts a hand under my elbow. My foot on his stirrup. Hups-a-daisy! Squeezing into the saddle. The poor mare staggers slightly under our weight.

But she's a tough old girl, and meets the challenge heroically.

"Who struck you?" Roland inquires. He speaks in a low voice, so as not to be heard. "Was it Isarn?"

"Yes."

"I'll have a talk with him this evening."

(Don't bother. What's the point?) "Forget it."

"Pagan—"

"Can't you see it'll just make things worse? Leave it alone, will you?"

He twists his head, trying to look at me. You can feel all the muscles hunching and sliding in his back.

"What's wrong?" he says. "What's the matter?"

"I'm a stupid, dirty, godless, cowardly Turk, that's what's the matter. You must have realized. Everyone else has."

"Pagan—"

Suddenly the sound of a horn echoes across the clearing. Roland stiffens. A murmur runs through the hunting party. "That's it!" Galhard exclaims. He puts his own horn to his lips and trumpets a reply. Jordan and Berengar and Joris follow suit. The dogs begin to howl.

Putting my hands to my ears.

"Hold on to me, Pagan!" (Roland's practically shouting.) "Don't let go, or you'll fall!"

Grabbing him around the waist as we lurch forward, Galhard in the lead, baying dogs running like a river around stamping hocks. Across the clearing and into the trees. Branches scraping and slapping. Horses stumbling.

God preserve us. This is going to be rough.

Put my head down and hold on tight. There's nothing else I can do, except keep my balance. Roland's not forcing the pace, because his mount's overloaded. Trailing behind the others. Struggling through to a second clearing, which is bigger than the first (mauve flowers glowing on yellowish grass), and swerving off westward. Following the dogs. Following the hunt. Trying to keep my balance.

This is all so confusing.

Jolt, jolt, jolt. The thud of hooves. Horns blaring. Roland's muscles tight and controlled: he's such a good rider. There's Jordan's back, up ahead. He's a good rider, too. Everyone is, except me. Jordan looks around and yells something, but it's impossible to hear.

Swerving, again.

More trees, but thinner this time. That would

make sense. I remember someone said that the object of the hunt is to force the stag out of its forest haunts and into open country. Jolt, jolt, jolt. I wonder how long this is going to last.

Slowing, suddenly. The dogs have stopped barking. Raise my head from Roland's back, and there's Isarn, waving his hands around. Where did he come from? What's happened?

"What happened, my lord?"

"Nothing." Roland's panting slightly. "It's a hart's ruse. We'll pick up the scent again in a moment."

"What ruse?"

"It retraces its steps and then leaps to one side, trying to break the scent."

Poor thing. How clever. But not clever enough. Isarn's leading the lymers around in ever-widening circles, urging them on with clucks and wordless shouts. Look across and see Berengar, drinking from a wineskin. God, but I could do with a drink. This sun is hot.

"How much longer, my lord?"

"What?" His mind is far away.

"How much longer will this take, do you think?"

"I don't know. That depends on the stag."

A dog's sharp, excited yap pierces the air. More

dogs join in. Isarn shouts something at Galhard, who wheels his horse around, kicking it forward.

And the hunt continues.

Riding, riding, riding. On and on. Across a track. Through a stream. Up the slippery bank on the other side. Roland's voice: "Come on, girl! Come on!" Aimery tries to jump it, and ends up in the water. (I hope he drowns.) More scrub and slapping branches. Sweat stinging my eyes.

There's nothing fun about this. This is terrible. I feel as if my head's going to come off.

"There! There!" Someone screaming. Joris? Surely not. Look up and get a stick in the eye.

"Ah! Ah!" Let go of Roland and nearly fall off. Grab him again. He clutches my wrist.

"What?" he exclaims.

"It's my eye—"

"Is it bad?"

"I don't think so."

All at once, the most hideous noise. Like the fall of Jericho. Dogs howling. Horns trumpeting. People shouting.

The sound of a stag at bay.

‡CHAPTER THIRTEEN‡

What a mess. What confusion. Baying dogs and bleating horns and a knot of milling horses, all sweating, all wild-eyed, all trying to jostle each other out of the way. Roland bringing up the rear, circling the crowd, dodging trees and clumps of bush.

And suddenly, there it is. The stag.

By God, but it's big. Look at its antlers! Bucking and diving. Charging and retreating. Its neck streaked with foam and blood, its flanks shiny with sweat. The dogs are all around it, teeth bared, hackles raised, yellow-eyed. When it lowers its head, they back off, yipping. One of them darts forward, snapping at its haunch. *Crack!* A leg shoots out and the dog catches a terrific blow on its skull.

"Roland! Roland!" Berengar makes some sort of signal. Why's he dismounting? Roland shifts in front of me.

"Take the reins," he gasps. "I'm getting down."

"But—"

Whoops! There he goes. Throwing me the reins as our mare shies and whinnies. Nervous, poor thing: it's the noise and the smell of blood. Shouts of encouragement as Roland draws his sword. Berengar draws his own almost simultaneously. And there's Jordan, in his brilliant Italian brocade (so impractical, yet somehow so appropriate), a long and beautiful blade in his hand, following Roland around the snapping circle of dogs.

Berengar moves in the opposite direction.

What are they doing? I don't understand. All three of them so intent, so absorbed, as smooth as ducks on the wing, each one's actions either linked to or mirrored in the actions of the others. It's like watching a single person split in three as they station themselves around the frantic stag: Berengar in front, Roland and Jordan behind. The tension's so bad, I feel as if I'm going to be sick.

Berengar. He lunges. The stag ducks and whirls,

charging at him, tossing its head. He leaps back, moves sideways. The stag follows, jabbing, retreating, jabbing again. It doesn't see Jordan. It's too busy with Berengar. Jordan edges up behind, carefully, carefully, the dogs scattering, the stag grunting, and Jordan, so close, his face as cool as dew, his sword catching the sunlight . . .

There! It's so quick! What did he do? He cut something in the hart's hind leg. It screams and lurches (oh, God, poor thing), swings around, staggers, crippled in one leg, blood on its rump, throwing itself at Jordan, who jumps back and catches his heel. Falls. Rolls. One arm shielding his face from the thrashing antlers.

But Roland's there. Raising his sword over his head, both hands on the hilt, and—

WHUMP!

Brings it down like an axe between the horns and the neck. Cutting the spine. Through the marrow.

Ending the agony.

Everything dissolves in a wash of tears. I don't know why—this is crazy—it's just an animal. It's dead. That's nothing to cry about. But I'm so confused . . . maybe it's not the stag. Maybe it's the way they actually did it. All together like that, so perfect and assured.

Scrubbing the tears away, to look at the blood-soaked earth under the yawning wound. It's dead, all right. And there's Berengar, whooping, his arms around Roland. Galhard, slapping Jordan on the back. Jordan, his neck scratched and bloody, ruffling Roland's hair. Everyone grinning. Everyone excited. A confused babble of voices, as everyone tries to make himself heard.

Except me. I've got nothing to say. I don't belong here. Gazing up at the sky, which is high and bleached and silent, with faint streaks of distant cloud and a lazy bird, hovering, drifting like a tuft of down in the breeze.

"Why are you crying?"

It's Foucaud. Still in the saddle, leading Jordan's palfrey. Mind your own business, Beanstalk.

"I'm not crying."

"Yes you are."

"I'm not!" Dismounting, to avoid his bug-eyed stare. So dizzy! God! And the side of my face hurts. Resting my forehead on the mare's sticky flank. If only I could lie down somewhere.

"Look, Pagan!" This time it's Roland, striding

toward me. His face is as bright as silver: below it, his crimson tunic is heavy, almost black, with blood. "Look, Pagan. Lord Galhard gave me the hart's right foot."

Well, stuff me with saffron. Isn't that exciting.

"Because it's been six whole years since last time, and I acquitted myself with honor," he continues. Is this really Roland? It doesn't even sound like him. "Look Pagan, look at the size of it."

Looking obediently. One sawed-off cloven hoof. Sinews trailing.

"Very nice."

He frowns, a shadow creeping across his radiant features. "What's wrong?" he says.

"My head hurts."

"Where?" And he reaches for the throbbing, stiffening side of my face. But his hand is thick with gore. Caked with it. I can't help flinching.

"What did I do?" he says. "I didn't touch it."

"Don't. Just don't."

"There's a bruise coming up. It's only a bruise. We'll rinse it in bay oil when we return."

"*Roland!*" (He staggers as Berengar jumps on his back.) "Roly-poly! That's my boy, eh? Eh?" Berengar grabbing him around the neck. Rumpling his hair with blood-tacky fingers. "Still haven't lost

156

the old touch, have you, Roly? One blow and it's done. Been practicing on the Turks?"

"Something like that."

"This boy's no eunuch! This boy's got balls to spare!" Berengar punches Roland playfully in the ribs. "What do you say we get you a woman? Hmmm? Just to round off the day. Lots of nice girls, if you know where to look."

"Thanks, but I think not."

"Come on, Rolls! You're a man now!"

"No, I can't."

"Forget the Templars! Enjoy yourself! This isn't Jerusalem!" Roland grins sheepishly. Jordan appears beside him, something dangling from his long, fastidious fingers. "Anyone for a scrotum?" he inquires. "Or should we send it to the Abbot?" Berengar bursts out laughing.

Look at them. The three of them. Towering above the rest of us, with their clear blue eyes and their identical noses and the same folds in their cheeks when they smile. Blood-spattered. Sweat-soaked.

Why can't I bear to look at them?

"Oi, Pagan." Isoard appears. Standing there with his teeth bared, his hands behind his back. "Isarn thought you'd better take this."

What? What are you talking about?

"Hold out your hand," he says.

And let you chop it off? No thanks.

"Hold out your hand, Pagan, or you'll get my surprise in the face!"

Holding out my hand, reluctantly. He produces his own hand, piled high with something grayish and bloody and formless. *Splat!* Into my palm.

"Isarn said you'd probably need these brains. Since you don't have any of your own."

Looking down at the warm, quivering mass. Berengar's laughter booming in my ears.

Suddenly losing control of my stomach.

"Uh-oh! Stand clear, everyone!" (Berengar.) "Upwind, please!"

Oh, God. Oh, God. Retching and heaving. Groaning. Gasping. I'm going to die. I'm just going to die. Mess all over the ground. All over my boots. Don't know where the vomit ends and the brains begin.

"Well, Isoard." Jordan's unmistakable drawl. "That'll teach you to throw meat at people, won't it?"

Oh, good. Did I hit Isoard? Well aimed, Pagan. On my knees now, exhausted, with Roland's hand on my head. Everyone else has moved away (even the poor old horse). Looking up, and there's the

158

carcass. On its back, half-flayed, its hide propped up at the corners with little sticks so that the blood won't run off. Isarn working away at the belly, hauling out reams and reams of intestines. Other people hacking off limbs.

Jesus. I feel so sick.

"It must be the sun." Roland's voice seems to come from a long way off. "Or the blow to your head. Just lie down in the shade for a while. We should be leaving soon."

"I'm so thirsty."

"I'll get you a drink."

He wanders away, tossing the severed foot from hand to hand. What's he going to do with that, I wonder? Eat it? The dogs are gathered around what's left of their kill, whining, pleading, as Isarn and Joris and Isoard pull it to pieces exactly like ants. The guts in one sack. The head in another. Limbs wrapped up like babies' corpses. Blood drained off into leather bottles.

They really know what they're doing.

"Here." A leather bottle, thrust in my face. Roland's returned. "Drink this."

"It's not—it's not blood, is it?"

"Blood? Of course not. It's wine."

Very warm wine. Clawing at my throat like a

159

Turkish mace as it goes down. Not the smoothest drop I've ever sampled.

"Perhaps I'd better not."

"Too rich?"

"You could say that."

"I'll see if I can find some water."

He disappears again, his step buoyant, his hair gleaming like gold in the sunlight. Some of the dogs are fighting over scraps of meat, but everywhere else it's happy faces and cheerful voices. Berengar, swigging wine. Jordan waving his stag's scrotum. Galhard laughing with Aimery. Isarn beaming as he wallows around in the stag's rib cage. Everyone is talking as loudly as possible.

"Thought we'd lost it after the soiling."

"That Lionhead is worth her weight in gold!"

"Keep the bladder, boy. You can't beat stag's urine for poultices."

"Did you see the way Lord Jordan jumped that last gully? Like a bird. He could ride his way to heaven."

All the merry babble. And here am I, dirty, stinking, ill, ignorant, with a sore head and a split lip, sitting in a pool of my own vomit.

I've never felt so alone in all my life.

"Cheer up, Pagan." Roland again, this time with

160

a wineskin full of water. "Foucaud says you can keep this until we get back. Wash your face. You'll feel better if you do."

That sounds unlikely. It'll take more than a clean face to lift my spirits. But what's the good of arguing?

The water tastes faintly of wine and sweat.

"Can you stand? Yes? Lord Galhard wants to leave now. He wants to get back before dark. You'll be able to make it, won't you?"

"Yes, my lord." Taking his hand, as he hauls me upright. All around, people are springing into saddles—some more lightly than others. Aimery seems to be limping. Joris grunts and groans. But Roland leaps onto his horse's back without effort, as fresh as a spring dawn, strong and serene. He pulls me up behind him as if I were made of feathers.

"What you really need is a good, long rest," he says. "You just didn't get enough sleep last night. You'll be all right tomorrow."

"If you say so, my lord."

Galhard's already mounted and moving off into the sun. He keeps the pace slow because the horses are all tired out. Blood drips from the warm, heavy bags tied to their saddles, and the dogs scuffle and snap as they fight over each drop. Suddenly, from

the end of the straggling column, someone begins
to sing:

"He sang to me and bade me follow
Down the meadow path to where the roses fade
And laid me down in a grassy hollow
On a flow'ry bed of woven lilies that he'd made."

Is it Foucaud? Surely not. I didn't know he could
sing so well. Heads turn, and the horses flick their
ears as other voices join in: Isarn's, thin and high;
Aimery's, loud and raw; Berengar's, like the sound
of bagpipes passing through a goat's stomach:

"He sang to me and bade me kiss him.
Sweet as honeysuckle, his soft lips met mine.
He asked if I would surely miss him
And my heart still sings with gladness at our love divine."

The lazy chorus drifts across the sunny land-
scape like a wisp of smoke, and the leaves rustle,
and the insects buzz, and all at once Roland's rib
cage swells, almost breaking my grip, to accom-
modate the air that he proceeds to use in a way
that I've never heard him use it before.

He begins to sing:

"He sang to me of his desire
Down there in the hollow where I laid my head
And spoke to me with words of fire
As gentle breezes sighed upon our flow'ry bed."

I don't believe it. This can't be true. Roland Roucy de Bram? Singing a dirty troubadour ballad? His voice is softer than I would have expected, but rich and tuneful. Warm. Mellow.

Oh, God, it's so confusing. I don't understand. What's happening here? There's something going on, and I just can't work it out.

"He sang to me, my gentle lover,
There where flowers bloomed and where the larks sang sweet
But now it's cold and the spring is over
And I long for summer days when once again we'll meet."

"By the balls of Baal, but I'll be glad to get off this horse," Berengar adds, as the last, gentle note falls from the air. "I feel as if someone's been using my buttocks for a battering ram."

The sweet saints preserve us. If only someone would.

CHAPTER FOURTEEN

There are people waiting for Galhard in the hall. Three monks, all in Benedictine black, are perched like crows around the high table. The tallest seems to have something wrong with his eye: it's wet and inflamed, and he keeps dabbing at it with the corner of his sleeve. His neighbor has the face of a lizard, seamed and ancient, with a wide mouth, an almost invisible nose, and small, bright, expressionless black eyes. The third monk isn't much older than I am. He's the kind of wholly forgettable person you'd always be leaving behind by accident.

None of them looks like a match for Galhard.

"So," he says, erupting into the hall, "you're from the Abbot, are you?" His tone is grumpy, but not life-threatening. Yet.

"My lord," the tall monk replies, "we are brethren of Saint Jerome. I am Brother Humbert. This is Brother Norgaud. We have come here to represent our good father Abbot Tosetus, concerning a matter that has distressed him greatly."

As Galhard approaches the high table, large and heavy and smelling like a leper's armpit, Brother Humbert's voice falters a little. But Galhard's not after Humbert: he's after the wine. He swills down what's left and turns to Germain, who's been hovering at his elbow ever since we dismounted.

"More wine!" he barks. "Where's the food? What have you been doing, you lazy clods? I want something to eat, and I want it now!"

Ominous rumbling of agreement from Berengar, as he drops onto a bench by the door. Germain scurries off to the kitchen. Aimery unbuckles his sword belt, which he throws across one of the tables. *Clank!* And here's Jordan, his beautiful surcoat encrusted with dry blood, looking around for a place to collapse. He sees me and winks.

I don't understand Jordan. I don't understand why he's being so nice. Why did he offer to let

Foucaud rub down Roland's horse? So that I wouldn't have to do it myself? Or was it just to annoy Roland? It certainly *did* annoy him. But he had to accept Jordan's offer, in the end, because I happen to feel exactly like a pair of old riding breeches that someone's wrung out and beaten dry on a washboard.

The dogs creep in and throw themselves onto the rushes, too tired even to sniff around for scraps. Some of them fall asleep; some lick their wounds. Galhard deposits his great bulk on one of the high-backed chairs and stretches his legs out in front of him.

"Well?" he growls. "Let's get on with it. I've been hunting all day, and I'm tired. What does the Abbot want to tell me?"

"My lord," says Humbert in a high voice, "two of our brethren, Brother Raoul and Brother Guibert, were lodging with Father Puy of Bram last night. Brother Raoul arrived back at the abbey around noon, alone. He told us that Brother Guibert had been abducted. By you, my lord."

A pause. Galhard waits. Humbert begins to perspire.

"Father Puy actually identified you, my lord," he

continues. "It seems that you and your sons were responsible."

"One moment, Brother," Roland interrupts. "You should tell the Abbot that I was not involved. I am Lord Roland and I had nothing to do with it."

"Shut up, Roland." (Standard response from Galhard, who doesn't even turn his head.) "If you want to know where your friend is, Brother Humbert, I can tell you right now. He's under your feet, in one of our cellars. And he's going to stay there until the Abbot releases my man. So you can relay that message to the Abbot. His man for mine. A fair bargain."

Humbert dabs at his eye, at his top lip, at his rosy, balding skull, which glistens in the torch-light. "My lord," he says carefully, "the man in the Abbot's custody is a criminal and a heretic. Brother Guibert, on the other hand, has committed no offense. His confinement is an injustice that cries out to God."

"Look, Brother, I don't care if I've got a saint or a demon down there. That's irrelevant. All I'm concerned about is my jurisdiction." Galhard leans forward and practically drills a hole in the tabletop with his index finger. "If your Abbot wants his monk back, he knows what to do. An exchange. Understand?"

Suddenly Norgaud speaks. His voice is the voice of a snake, soft and sibilant. "The Abbot regrets that if you don't surrender Brother Guibert, he will ask the Bishop that you be excommunicated, and your lands be subject to an interdict," he declares. "As you may know, our Holy Father Pope Lucius, may he rest in peace, announced four years ago that all receivers and defenders of heretics shall be subjected to the same punishment as heretics. The Abbot believes that you have publicly, and without shame, encouraged and favored certain people of false beliefs who even now enjoy the benefits of your protection. Therefore you should abjure your errors, make satisfaction, and return to the unity of the Catholic faith, or suffer the condemnation of perpetual anathema."

Perpetual who? I didn't quite catch all of that. Galhard bursts out laughing.

"I'm sorry, but I don't understand," Jordan drawls. "Am I correct in thinking that you just made some kind of *threat*, Brother Norgaud?"

"My lord, this is not a laughing matter." Roland moves toward the high table, frowning. "Forgive me, my lord, but this is serious."

"Why?" says Berengar. "What's a perpetual anathema? Some kind of siege machine?"

Galhard is still shaking his head and wiping his eyes. He moans in appreciation. "Oh—oh—what a joke," he splutters. "What a joke. The Abbot waves his deadly perpetual anathema, and strong men crumble."

"My lord—" Roland begins. But he's cut short by Humbert.

"There's also the question of our mill, my lord," Humbert adds quietly. And Galhard stiffens.

"What about the mill?"

"My lord, if you don't return Brother Guibert, the abbey will be forced to prevent your vassals from using our mill. No one from Bram will be admitted."

Gulp. That's done it. The laughter leaves Galhard's face. The blood gathers in his eyes. He bares his teeth like a leopard.

"My lord—" says Roland. But he's too late. Galhard pounces, grabbing Humbert's collar and jerking him halfway across the table. Shaking him like a dog shaking a rat. "You slimy leech!" he roars. "I'll kick your brains out!"

"My lord!" Roland seizes his arm. "No, my lord, no!"

"You're dog meat! Do you hear me? You're dead and digested!" Galhard drags Humbert right off the table, onto the floor. Begins to pull him toward the stairwell. But Roland's hanging off one arm, and Norgaud off the other: they're slowing him down. "You'll be joining Guibert in the grain vat!" he bellows.

"My lord! Reconsider!" Roland cries. "There's another solution—"

"Get out of my way!"

"My lord, you can't do this—"

"Get out of my way or get out of this castle!"

"Wait." It's Jordan, suddenly appearing beside Galhard. "We don't really have the space to hold four monks, my lord," he remarks quietly. "Perhaps we should consider our alternatives. Perhaps we should listen to what Roland has to say."

Perhaps we should what? Pardon me while I pick up my eyeballs. Am I hearing things? Roland looks stunned. Even Galhard looks stunned. "What?" he says.

"If I could just have a quick word, my lord," Jordan continues. "In private."

Galhard stares at Jordan for a moment, and comes to a decision. He releases his grip on

170

Humbert, who subsides onto the floor with a groan. He jerks his arm out of Roland's grasp. He pushes Norgaud away. "All right," he grunts. "Make it fast, though. In here." And he leads Jordan into his sleeping chamber.

The door slams.

"Well," says Berengar, as everyone exchanges looks. "You were damn lucky. I could have sworn you were heading for the chop there, Brother."

"Manus Dei," Norgaud murmurs, helping Humbert to his feet. *"Te Deum laudamus."* Humbert doesn't reply: he's speechless with shock and panting like a hound. Roland looks worried.

Suddenly the food arrives.

"Ha!" Berengar spies it first. "At last!" He springs to his feet, pouncing on the bread in Germain's basket. Segura is carrying a jug of wine and a bowl of olives. There also seems to be a kind of long dumpling, cut into disks, and a round of cheese on a platter.

Berengar whips out his hunting knife.

"Where's Lord Galhard?" Germain asks anxiously. He sets his burden down carefully on the table. "Should I take him some food?"

"He's in there," Berengar mumbles through a

mouthful of bread. He's pointing at the closed door. But even as he speaks, it opens, and Galhard's head appears.

"Roland!" The head jerks. "I want you."

Hello. Now what? This is all very peculiar. Roland touches my arm. "Go to bed, Pagan." (In low tones.) "I'll be up when I'm ready."

Watching him move away. Let's just hope it's not an ambush. The monks are whispering together at one end of the table, as Berengar guzzles food at the other end. Well, I'm not hanging around here. Making for the stairwell. Groping up the stairs with my hand on the wall (why don't they light these damned stairs?), carefully, slowly, because there might be spilled wax. Or oil. Or something even nastier.

Lady Gauzia's in her room. You can hear her talking to someone. Tayssiras? The light spills out through her door, warm and welcoming. If only *I* had a wife. And a nice bed. And a chest to put my clothes in. Jordan doesn't realize how lucky he is.

Forgot to bring a candle. Oh, well, there's light enough from Gauzia's door. Light enough to see Roland's chain mail, lying where I left it on the floor of our room. And there's his uniform . . . and his shield . . . and the pile of straw . . .

The pile of *straw*?

God curse it! My bed! My blanket! No one's brought them in yet! God curse it, they must still be sitting out in the bailey, where we left them to dry. Well, I'm damned if I'm going to get them now. Someone else can do it. I'm not moving another step.

Collapsing onto the pile of straw, my head throbbing like a giant pimple. God, God, God, I feel as if I'm going to faint. Eyes shut. The pain in my head and my cheekbone. Where's Roland? Doesn't he care? I'm ill, damn you! Why don't you come? I need something cold on my face. I need— what was it? Bay oil? I need herb tea.

Straw is so uncomfortable. I hate it, I hate everything here. Thinking about Jerusalem. Thinking about dates. I love dates. Stuffed dates, in syrup. Loaf sugar. Apples of Paradise, long and yellow. Food stands, in the Street of Flowers. Night watch. Cock fights. Money changers. Bervold, spitting . . . and the alleys, down by Saint Anne . . . fires . . . blue . . . going far . . . planks . . . the ship lurches . . . grab the gold, it's turning into water . . .

"Pagan!"

Wha—? Who—? Roland? Was I asleep?

"Pagan." He's crouching beside me, holding a

candle. Prodding my arm. "Good news, Pagan. It's good news."

That voice. It doesn't sound like Roland's voice. It sounds too . . . too . . . rubbing my eyes, just to make sure. Oh, yes, it's Roland. But there's something strange about his face. A kind of glow. Is it the candle? I've never seen—he looks exultant. Exultant. That's the only way to describe it. So peaceful, so content, so elated.

"My father has agreed to release Brother Guibert," he announces. And his voice rings like a bell. "He has decided that the cost of detaining the monks would be far too high."

"Really?" Propping myself up on one elbow. Trying to sound interested. "That's very odd. I wouldn't have expected that at all. Are you sure he's serious?"

Roland laughs. He actually laughs. I can't believe it. I've never heard him laugh before, not ever. What's happened? Is he drunk? Am I hallucinating?

"Poor Pagan. Of course he's serious. I told him that I would take the matter to the Bishop myself. Or to the Templars, if need be. I told him that he was the injured party, and that with my help he would have no trouble convincing anyone that his cause was just." Roland's hand suddenly closes on mine, squeezing hard. "He listened to me, Pagan. He agreed with me. He accepted my arguments."

Hell in a hand basket. So that's what this is all about. Looking up into his dazzling face, with its flushed brow and sparkling eyes and flashing teeth. Feeling the radiance of his joy like the warmth of a blazing fire.

"I'm glad, my lord. I'm very glad for you."

He squeezes my hand again, so hard that he almost breaks my fingers. (Ow! Ouch!) Releasing them just in time, as he pats my shoulder and rises to his feet. "You go to bed, Pagan. I know how tired you are. Don't worry about waking up early. You can sleep for as long as you like."

Well, that's something. He really must be in a good mood. Listening as he putters around, unbuckling his sword belt, pulling off his boots, washing his face and hands. I've never heard him humming before, either. It sounds like another of those troubadour songs. I suppose he must have learned it as a child, along with all the others. Odd that I've never heard him sing them until today. But then again, maybe—

Maybe I've never seen him happy until today.

A sinking feeling. Could that be true? But it's

terrible! Surely he must have been happy before? Thinking back, right back to the first time he ever smiled at me, on pilgrimage escort. To that lovely, sunny day when we sailed into Marseille, past Gorgonassa and the Tower of Saint John, and looked out at the walls and the people and the fishing boats (such a busy, peaceful, prosperous scene). To that glorious ride from Maugio to Béziers, when we found that field of golden flowers, and raced our horses all the way across to the stream on the other side. Surely he was happy then? I was happy then.

But I suppose it's different for Roland. He has a family. I've never had anyone, except him.

And I'm beginning to wonder if I even have him anymore.

‡CHAPTER FIFTEEN‡

It's a big room, with windows, and the sea beyond. I think it must be a dormitory. There's my bed, and that's Joscelin's bed, and someone's grooming a dog in the sunlight. Can't see his face, but he's covered in gold. Golden rings. Golden fingernails. Turn away, and here's Tayssiras, waiting.

Her hair is loose, and she's wearing a long yellow robe, laced up the sides. Her arms are bare. As she lifts them over her head, you can see her nipples through the fabric. Reaching out—she's smiling— but the dog barks.

Raf! Raf-raf-raf-raf!

Open my eyes. I can still hear that dog, far away downstairs. Is it morning? It must be. Yes, I'm awake. I'm awake, and my face hurts, and I must have had another one of those stupid dreams.

At least I didn't make a mess, though.

Sitting up stiffly. Straw in my hair. Where's Roland? Is it late? How long have I been sleeping? Oh, that's right. Now I remember. He said he wouldn't wake me. And he must have pulled my boots off, too, because I certainly didn't. Dragging them over. Shoving my feet in. I really need new boots. These ones look as if they've been lying dead in a swamp for the last three hundred years.

Now, what am I supposed to do today? Horses, naturally. Boots. I have to drag the beds back in. Clean Roland's sword: I bet he only gave it a wipe, after that stag business. Probably needs a good polish. And what about the clothes he was wearing? Surely he didn't put them on again? No, there they are. I'll clean them, too.

"Good morning, Pagan."

Look up. It's Jordan. What's he doing here?

"Sleep well?" he inquires. "I hope so." He looks very sleek and fresh, and he's carrying Acantha on his wrist. "I was beginning to think that you'd never wake up."

"Is it late, my lord?"

178

"Well, it's not actually afternoon yet, but it's a bit late for breakfast. How is your head?"

"My head?" Touching it, gingerly.

Ouch.

"Come here," he says. "Into the light. Come." He catches my chin. Turns my face. Studies it. "Hmm. How unfortunate. I've had a little word with Isarn. He really should learn to take my warnings seriously. I think he will, from now on."

God preserve us. What's that supposed to mean?

"But I don't think you've suffered any permanent damage," Jordan continues. His hand feels smooth and cold, like marble. Moving away from it, carefully, so as not to cause offense.

"Have you seen Lord Roland, my lord?"

"Ah, yes, Lord Roland." He smiles, in a rather unpleasant fashion. "Lord Roland is a busy man. He's been busy all morning. First he had to bid farewell to our monastic visitors. Then he had to discuss certain issues with Lord Galhard and Lord Berengar. And with me, of course. In fact I believe he's still with the others." (Jordan's so big, he seems to fill the doorway. Isn't he going to let me through? What's he trying to accomplish?) "I must confess that I'm not really interested in the

Crusade. But my father always likes to thrash everything out—"

"You mean they're discussing the Crusade?"

"Naturally. Isn't that why you're here?"

Well, stuff me with chestnuts. So they've finally gotten down to business! Roland must have seen it coming last night: no wonder he was so happy. Especially if he thought that his father might take up the Cross after all. But if Galhard does take up the Cross, that means we'll have to stay here. Unless—

"Pagan. *Pagan.* Did you hear me? I asked you a question."

"Oh, sorry."

"Would you like to join me in the western paddock? I'm training Acantha. I could do with some help."

So that's why he won't get out of my way. Looking at Acantha, who's sitting there like a little, gleaming statue, all talons and beak. Looking from her to Jordan. He's all talons and beak, too.

"My lord, I have chores to finish—"

"They can wait."

"But Lord Roland—"

"Don't worry about Lord Roland."

"But—"

"What? But what?" He leans closer. "What did he tell you about me? Hmm? What did he tell you? Pagan?"

Gulp.

"Nothing, my lord."

"Now, Pagan, do you think I'm a fool? Do you think I don't know what's going on in your head? Of course I do. In fact I know exactly what he told you. He told you to stay away from me, didn't he?"

Oh, hell. I'm sick of this. Why worry about his feelings? He probably doesn't even have any.

"Yes, my lord, as a matter of fact, he did."

"And did he say why?"

"He told me about a hawk you once killed."

"I see." And he does, too. His eyes glint as he remembers. "So you'd prefer to stay away from me, in case I put out your eyes with a hot stick? Is that it?"

"Of course not."

"Why, then?"

"Because I do what I'm told!"

"Pagan." Suddenly he frowns. His tone becomes serious. "Has it occurred to you that my problem is with Roland? I've nothing against you. I like you.

181

I enjoy your company. And I don't regard you as another part of Roland, because you're quite clearly an individual in your own right. So my relations with him don't have anything to do with what happens between you and me. Do you understand that?"

God preserve us. Gnawing my thumbnail.

"But of course you understand," he says. "You understand a lot more than most people realize. That's why I enjoy your company. It makes a change from the morons I usually have to put up with."

"My lord—"

"Yes?" I can't stand the way he stares. Ease off, will you? It's not my fault. I can't help it.

"My lord, I don't even know how to train a hawk. I've never tried."

"Oh, don't worry about that. There's nothing to it. All you have to do is learn the call notes." He moves away from the door, his eyes still boring a hole through my skull. "Coming? Come on, you might enjoy yourself."

Well, I might, mightn't I? Where's the harm in it? If I take my sword, I shouldn't have any problems. Especially since he isn't wearing his own sword.

"What are you doing?" he says as I buckle myself

into my sword belt. "You won't need that—the meat's already cut."

"I never go anywhere without it, my lord."

He smiles and shrugs, and heads for the stairwell. There's no one in Berengar's room. The stairs are empty. Lady Gauzia's sitting with Tayssiras at the high table, crumbling a piece of bread between her fingers. She looks up, and looks away. Jordan walks past as if she isn't even there.

But Tayssiras dimples at me and waves her hand. Don't blush, Pagan. Don't think about that dream. She looks very bright and healthy next to Gauzia, whose face is all bones and shadows.

I wonder where Roland is. In Galhard's sleeping chamber? Can't see him because the door's shut.

"You may have heard me whistling the call notes," Jordan remarks, as we emerge into the bailey. "There are only three of them, so they're not hard to remember." And he whistles a familiar little tune, several times. "Can you do that? Let me hear you."

Well, you certainly don't have to be King Solomon to master this one. He listens carefully and seems satisfied with my attempt. "That's the most important thing," he points out. "All you have to do is remember those notes and follow my orders."

Moving toward the gate, past the decrepit old barracks and the kitchen. There's Bernard, lumbering along with a sack of flour. There's Ademar, relieving himself against a wall. And who's this, emerging from the stables? It can't be Isarn?

God preserve us. What happened to his face?!

He sees Jordan and stops. There's a nasty gash across his left eyelid. His eye is swollen shut, and he obviously can't breathe through his nose. Could it be broken? He retreats into the stables, quickly.

Jordan doesn't even spare him a glance.

"My lord—"

"Yes, Pagan?"

On second thought, I don't want to ask. "Nothing."

It's a sultry kind of day, with a threat of thunderstorms in the air. Smoke drifts sluggishly from the chimneys of Bram. The sound of a bell in the distance.

Past the sentry, across the bridge and turn right. Hello, fresh hoof-marks. Left by the monks, I suppose.

"It isn't far," says Jordan. "It's just beyond those trees. We'll have to make sure that the sheep stay out of our way." He begins to make clucking noises as Acantha flaps her wings restlessly. "Hush, beautiful. Hush, my girl. We're nearly there."

Birds cheeping, insects buzzing. Dandelions. Horse dung. Butterflies. Stomping through the grass behind Jordan, as the sheep look up to stare at us dully. A few plaintive bleats from the lambs.

"This should do," Jordan suddenly announces. "The grass isn't too high here." He turns to me, his face intent and serious. "Now, Pagan, do you see the little bags on my belt? I want you to take that one, because there's meat in it. The other one contains the lure. You can take that out, too."

The lure? What's that? Fishing around obediently, dragging out a pair of bird's wings tied to a piece of meat.

"First of all, I want you to remove her hood," Jordan continues. "Then I want you to let her taste the meat on that lure. Just give her a taste—don't let her eat it. Then I want you to move away until I tell you to stop. Is that clear?"

"Yes, my lord."

"All right. Let's begin, then."

The hood's made of leather, tied under her chin. Jordan whistles the call notes as her huge, startled eyes are uncovered; she flaps her wings, and the bells tinkle on her jesses. Jordan holds on to them firmly.

Here, Acantha. Look at the nice lure. Mmmm, delicious.

"That's enough," Jordan says. "She's had enough. Back away now. Keep the lure in her line of vision. That's it. You're doing well. Keep going. Stop."

Stop. The hawk's eyes are fixed on my lure. What do I do next? Jordan's standing as motionless as a statue, his free hand clasping a long cord tied to the end of Acantha's leash.

"Good. That's good," he says. "Now I'm going to ask you to put the lure down and move away slowly. Don't distract her. When she pounces on the lure, take a piece of meat from the bag I gave you and put it down close to her. Make sure you whistle the call notes while you're doing it, or she'll get nervous. Then, when she's moved to the new meat, I want you to pick her up on the line. But let her eat the meat first. Understand?"

Of course I understand. "Yes, my lord."

"Do it."

Putting the lure down, carefully. Moving away, carefully. Two steps. Three steps. Four steps. Five.

"Stop," says Jordan, and lets go of Acantha's jesses. She springs into the air and glides down to the lure, feet first. Yes! Right on target. "Now!" Jordan cries. "Not too fast!"

Not too fast. Take it easy, Pagan. Whistling the call notes. Come on, Acantha. Look at this lovely bit of gristle, all by itself on the ground. Come on, then. Come on, sweetheart. It's all just for you.

She flaps her wings, clumsily, and moves toward the meat, half walking, half flying. That's the way. Eat up, Acantha. Her talons close on the bloody scrap as she tears at it with her beak. I wonder if it's a bit of that stag from yesterday.

"All right," says Jordan. "You can pick her up now. Bring her back here, and watch that beak."

I'm watching, I'm watching. But she's a good-natured girl, and keeps her beak to herself. What a beautiful creature. Holding her like a chicken, one hand on each wing. Jordan's waiting with his arm extended.

"She's smart, my lord."

"Of course she is."

"Is it the first time she's done this?"

"The very first time."

"Aren't you a clever bird?" Stroking the silky feathers on her neck. "Are we going to try again, my lord?"

"If you want to."

"Yes please!" Look up, and he's smiling, but it's a pleasant smile. "Should I move farther away this time?"

"By all means."

"She'll probably end up carrying off one of those lambs, if we're not careful!"

Suddenly, a shout. Distant, but quite clear. It sounds like Roland's voice.

"Pagan!"

And there he is, approaching through the trees. Dressed in something blue and gold that I haven't seen before. (One of Jordan's tunics?) He stops and jerks his arm. Come here, Pagan.

"My lord—"

"Yes, yes. I understand." Jordan's smile fades. "Off you go, then. Mustn't keep Roland waiting."

I can hear his footsteps behind me as I head for the trees, toward Roland. It seems like a very long walk. Roland's standing with his hands on his hips; there's something ominous about the set of his shoulders, and his face is lost in shadow. But gradually, as the distance closes, his features emerge, and they're not a pretty sight. All the radiance has disappeared. His expression is stony, his eyes like glass.

Make haste, O God, to deliver me; make haste to help me, O Lord.

"I'm sorry, my lord, I was helping with the falcon—"

"Come," he snaps, and turns away. Better do as he says. Look back at Jordan, who's smiling again. "You mustn't blame the boy," Jordan declares. "He was under orders." But Roland doesn't respond.

He just keeps walking, his strides so long and vigorous I almost have to run to keep up.

"My lord—wait—I'm sorry, but he asked me. What's wrong, my lord? Please don't be angry—"

"It was a trick," he says.

"What?"

"It was a trick. All of it." His voice is harsh. "When I left my father, I went to the stables to look for you. Berengar's battle mount was gone. So was Jordan's. And so were Aimery and Joris. They must have taken them."

"You mean—"

"They went after the monks. Aimery and Joris and Pons. While my father talked. While you were asleep. It was all a trick, to prevent us from stopping them."

Jesus. "Do you think—?"

"I don't know what to think." He's staring blankly at the ground ahead of him, crushing the flowers under heavy boots as he walks. "We're probably too late, but we must try," he says. "We must try to catch up. I don't know what they plan to do, but whatever it is, we have to move fast.

"We must try to stop this thing before it happens."

‡ CHAPTER SIXTEEN ‡

Lightning flickers against the brooding black clouds to the east. You can feel moisture in the air, but no rain yet. I just hope it holds off while we're still on the road. There's nothing worse than riding through a thunderstorm.

"My lord?"

Roland grunts. He's hardly said a thing since we left Bram. Not that it's easy to exchange words when you're trying to force the pace like this. But you can't keep a palfrey trotting forever, and sometimes you have to slow down just to give the animal a rest.

Then you can manage some kind of conversation, if your companion's in the mood.

"Did you say anything to Lord Galhard, my lord? About the missing horses?"

Roland nods but remains silent.

"And what did Lord Galhard say?"

"He denied any knowledge of their whereabouts."

"Hmmm."

Distant thunder echoes across the horizon. My head feels as if it's under siege, as if someone is sitting just in front of my left ear, hammering at my skull with an iron-plated mallet. It's a miracle that my brain still works under these conditions. Anyone else's brain would have packed up and moved off to a desert hermitage long ago.

"Do you know what I think, my lord?" (Just in case you're interested.) "I think that if something does happen, Lord Galhard will probably deny that he had anything to do with it. He'll probably say that it was done by brigands. It would explain why he didn't pursue the monks himself." It would also explain why he chose Aimery and Joris for the job. Of course! I understand now. "When you think about it, my lord, those monks never met either Joris or Aimery. Both of them were out hunting when the monks arrived, and both of them kept well out of the way when we all got back. Which means that if any of the monks do survive, they won't be able to identify their attackers as people who live at Bram. You see? And of course, yes, of course . . ." (Everything fits together.) "It makes sense, my lord, because with your father and brothers busy around the castle, there was nothing to arouse your suspicions, either. If any of them had been missing, you would have wondered where they were—"

"Instead of which, I had to wait until I entered the stables and noticed the empty stalls," Roland interrupts. "Something which you should have done already."

His voice is sharp. Forbidding. Strange.

"My lord—"

"If you'd obeyed my instructions and kept away from Jordan, you would have gone to the stables and seen the missing horses much earlier. We would have had a better chance of stopping this thing. But you played right into his hands, despite the fact that I warned you, specifically, to avoid him."

God preserve us. Could that be true? Could it all have been a trick, just to keep me out of the stables? Possibly. Probably. But somehow . . . I don't know. . . .

"My lord, I realize that Lord Jordan was part of this plan—"

193

"Part of it?!" Roland exclaims. "Jordan was the source of it! This whole business was his doing."

"Not entirely, my lord. Be fair. Lord Galhard was the one who kept you distracted, talking about the Crusade—"

"And Jordan was the one who lured you out of the castle, so that I had to spend even more precious time trying to find you. He was using you, Pagan, the way he uses everybody. Didn't I tell you not to trust him?"

Oh, right. So I'm just a fool. I'm a complete cesshead who doesn't know what he's doing, and who gets pushed around like a wheelbarrow. Well, thanks very much, Roland, that's really encouraging.

"My lord, I'm not stupid, you know. I do have the ability to judge people." He opens his mouth, but I'm too quick for him. "Lord Jordan has always been perfectly pleasant to me. He's even helped me out a few times, and he didn't gain anything from doing that. Has it occurred to you—I mean, I know it's probably hard for you to see this—but has it occurred to you that he might actually enjoy my company for its own sake? That we might actually get along? I realize I'm not very important, but am I such a waste of space that any attention I might get has to be the result of some—some vicious, underhanded plot?"

"In God's name!" (An oath! He used an oath! He's never used an oath!) "Open your eyes, Pagan! Can't you see what he's doing? Can't you see?" Surely this isn't Roland? Surely this isn't the Man of Marble? Fennel's ears flicker uneasily as Roland clenches his fists. "It's quite obvious what he's trying to do! He's trying to take you away from me! Just as he's tried to take everything else away, ever since we were children."

Oh, please. This is ridiculous. This is embarrassing.

"My lord, don't you think you're being a little—"

"It's true! It's true. You just don't understand. You don't know him. Everything he does is harmful. Everything he says is a lie." I've never seen Roland like this. Never. His face has gone to pieces. His voice is all over the place. "You might think he likes you, but he doesn't. He doesn't like anyone—especially me. He hates me. He hates me because my mother loved me the best. That's why he wants to take you away."

"My lord . . ." I can't believe this. Roland, what's happened to you? You're acting like a child. "My lord, he's never even asked me to leave your service. And if he did, I wouldn't go. What are you saying?"

A long pause. Roland stares down at his hands, flushed and speechless. *Splat. Splat. Splat-splat.* Oh, hell. Wouldn't you know it? The wilderness turneth into standing water, and dry ground into water springs.

Here comes the rain.

"My lord, I know you were very happy last night, because you thought that your father had faith in you." (Carefully, Pagan, tread carefully.) "Now you're disappointed. But you shouldn't let them upset you, my lord. They're not worth it." Looking across at his bowed head, as he wipes a drop of moisture from his cheek. Tears? No, rain. "You won't be blamed for their actions. And you shouldn't blame me, either. I'm very sorry that you've been treated so badly. If I can help you, I will. Because I'll always support you in everything, against everyone. I thought you understood that."

He raises his eyes. Opens his mouth. But something stops him from speaking: something up ahead. He stiffens and peers, his profile suddenly sharp and intent.

What? What is it?

Oh, I see. A shape on the road, lying there like a fallen bough. Still too far to see properly, but I don't like the look of it.

Roland kicks his horse into a canter.

Dense foliage on either side of us. Perfect for an ambush. Wait! My lord! But he's already slowed, his hand on his sword hilt, his gaze on the shadowy thickets of chestnut and blackthorn as he guides Fennel through a scattering of twigs and leaves and discarded possessions. A shoe. A buckle. A piece of bread. The raindrops are already turning dust into mud, but you can still see the pattern of attack and defense in the sudden confusion of hoof-marks.

"Stay there," says Roland. "Keep a lookout." He slides from his saddle and moves toward the long, motionless shape lying on its stomach in a sticky pool of blood. It's wearing a black habit. Roland puts out a hand, grabs a handful of wet robe, and turns the body over.

"Guibert," he says.

So that's Guibert. He's been chopped across the neck: his wound gapes like a second mouth. His head lolls. Blood everywhere. Blood and dirt.

Jesus.

"Pagan!" Roland's grim face, turned in my direction. "I told you to keep a lookout!"

197

Sorry. I'm sorry. Scanning the bushes, through a mist of rain. Glancing down the road. Leaves tremble. Lightning flashes. Coppertail snorts nervously.

"He's dead," says Roland. "Dead but still warm. May God have mercy on his soul." And he crosses himself.

"I can't believe they managed to catch up so fast." Raising my voice over the rumble of thunder. "How did they do it?"

"Cross-country. It's not difficult—there's a lot of grazing land between here and the castle. No water or plowed fields."

"Then they must have taken the same route back, or we would have met up with them."

Roland nods, straightens, and peers into the distance. His hair is wringing wet. "Can you see anything else?" he asks. "On the road?"

"No, my lord, nothing."

"The others must have got away. Unless they're lying dead in a bush somewhere." He begins to examine the scarred ground, walking, stopping, crouching, fingering, moving up the road step by careful step. Suddenly the steps grow faster: he seems to be following tracks. "Here," he calls.

"Here they are. All galloping. One, two, and here's three. Three horses, holding steady. . . ."

"With riders?"

"Perhaps. They kept to the road, anyway. That's a good sign."

"What about the fourth?"

"I don't know. Bolted? Stolen?"

"Surely even Joris wouldn't be stupid enough to take Guibert's horse?" Looking back over my shoulder, my voice sounds unnaturally loud. "It's too incriminating. Where would you hide it?"

Roland doesn't respond. He's retracing his steps, frowning because rain has begun to smudge and blur the prints.

Soon they'll have disappeared completely.

"I think the other three escaped," he says at last. "I don't believe they were followed. I think the engagement took place here, one man was killed, three escaped, and the attackers retired in the opposite direction. Perhaps Guibert was the only one they really wanted." He comes to where Guibert is lying, and stops. Bends over. Slides his hands under the limp body.

"My lord? What are you doing?"

He looks up, puzzled.

"What do you mean?" he says.

"My lord, you're not going to take him with us?"

"I can't just leave him where he is."

"But you have to." (Think, Roland, you're not thinking.) "We can't touch this, my lord. Any of it. If we do, we'll be implicated."

"What are you talking about? Don't be foolish."

"My lord, you're a member of the family. What will people think if you ride past with a dead monk dangling across your crupper?" Pause for a moment, to let the image sink in. He stares at me with blank, blue eyes. "They'll think you did it, my lord. They'll think you were involved."

"No." He shakes his head. "There were witnesses. I'm sure at least one is alive. People would know that I wasn't responsible."

"But they would also know who you are." Poor Roland. Standing there in the rain, spattered with mud, wearing gaudy, unsuitable clothes that don't fit him. He looks so lost and out of place. "My lord, consider what your father has done here. He's tried very hard to avoid linking your family with this murder. He's staged it outside his territory. He's used people unknown to the victims. He's obviously tried to make it look like the work of brigands. If you suddenly appear out of nowhere with Brother Guibert, people are going to start making connections."

"They'll do that anyway."

"Yes, but wouldn't it be better for everyone if brigands *were* held responsible? Otherwise this whole thing is going to escalate even more."

That's done it. I've hit the bull's-eye, there. He blinks and looks down at the body. Thinks for a moment before looking up at me again.

"So for the sake of keeping the peace," he murmurs, "this poor soul must be left here in the mud? Is that what you're saying?"

"My lord, the Abbot isn't going to let him lie here and rot. I'm sure that someone from the abbey will be sent to collect him." Glancing down the road, which is slowly disappearing under a network of puddles. "And we don't want to be here when they arrive."

Roland runs his hand through his dripping hair. "Then you think we should return to Bram?" he says.

"Well, of course." (What do you mean?) "Unless there's somewhere else we can go."

"I was thinking that we should report to the Temple at Carcassonne," Roland says, squelching toward his horse. "My father said that the Templars have a peacekeeping role in this country. If it is indeed an office of our Holy Rule, then perhaps we can seek help from the Preceptor, Commander Folcrand."

"Not today, though—it's too far."

"No, not today." He throws himself into the saddle, with less than his normal vigor. Perhaps the water is dragging him down. Or perhaps it's something else that weighs so heavily. "In any event, this is bad weather for riding," he continues. "I think I shall wait and see what happens. If my father is blamed—if the dispute gets any worse—I will go to Carcassonne. The Preceptor may have a solution."

He may, but I doubt it. As far as I can see, the best solution would be to lock all these murderers up in a box and let them fight it out between themselves. At least that way no one else would get hurt.

Roland brings Fennel's head around and circles Guibert's remains, just once, before drawing abreast of Coppertail. What a good rider he is. Every movement as smooth as silk.

"Pagan?" He turns to look at me. Hesitates. Proceeds. "I know only one prayer, 'Our Father.' It is the duty of all Templars to recite it every day, if they can."

"Yes, my lord, I know." (What's all this about?)

"But I'm not educated, and I don't think—" He pauses. "I don't think it's really appropriate. Not like . . . Do you remember the prayer that Esclaramonde recited? When her friend died? You said you knew it."

"It wasn't a prayer, my lord; it was a gospel."

"Do you remember the words?" His gaze shifts once more to Guibert's broken body. "I think we should say something."

Yowch! That's a tough one. Straining back to monastery mealtimes, with Brother Guige at the lectern. His creaky, rough voice, his hairy warts. Let's see. Let's see, now . . . ah yes, I remember.

"In the beginning was the Word, and the Word was with God, and the Word was God."

Roland bows his head and closes his eyes. Wet fustian clinging to my legs and arms, as the rain trickles into my collar.

"The same was in the beginning with God. All things were made by Him, and without Him was not anything made that was made."

Smell of wet earth, smell of wet horse. The rain gently washes Guibert's upturned face, cleaning the blood and dirt from his nose and mouth and eyelids.

"In Him was life, and the life was the light of

men. And the light shineth in darkness, and the darkness comprehended it not."

That's all I can remember. Silence descends, broken only by the patter of raindrops. Even the horses are still. Finally Roland opens his eyes, and crosses himself.

"Amen," he murmurs.

It's time to go.

CHAPTER SEVENTEEN

Thunk!

Roland's sword comes down hard on my shield. Whew! Just in time. Go for the gap. His blade parries, steel on steel, scraping. Shield up. Jump back. Move sideways.

"Good!" he pants. "Excellent!"

There! A breach! But he dodges away. Watch him. Watch him. Watch his foot.

"Watch that foot, Pagan. The feet are your guides. Where's your shield, boy? Up! Up! Do you think I'm aiming for your kneecaps?"

Thunk! Damn. He's always too quick. He surges forward, and it's time to retreat. In a shield-to-shield push, there won't be any contest.

"Good," he says. "Wait, what are you doing? The right flank, Pagan, look at it. No, sorry. Too late now."

Edging around the combat circle, looking for a hole in his defense. Feint to the right. He swings. There!

Clang!

My sword goes flying.

Laughter from Isoard, who's leaning against the stable wall. (Go boil your bowels, pus-bag.) But Roland seems quite pleased.

"Well done," he exclaims. "You had me working hard with that last attack." And he throws a forbidding glance at Isoard, who immediately falls silent.

Is that the sound of wheels, I can hear?

"Just remember to keep your shield high," Roland continues, turning back to me. "It's unlikely that I'll ever try to break your guard below the waist, from this height. I'd have to go groveling around on my knees to do that."

"My lord—"

"What you really need is someone with a similar build. A shorter reach would give you a tighter match, I think."

"Look, my lord." Pointing across the bailey, to

where a familiar wagon is creaking through the gates. Even from this distance you can see that Esclaramonde has come alone. Roland squints, frowning.

"Is that—?"

"Yes, my lord, it's Esclaramonde. I hope she's all right."

He drops his shield, which hits the cobbles with a hollow, wooden thud. Sheathes his sword. Wipes his sweaty palms on the skirts of his tunic.

Moves across to welcome her, his faithful squire at his heels.

Other people are emerging from various doorways, roused by the rattle of the cart. Segura. Germain. The stable boy. A spicy smell of cooking mingles with the scent of a brand-new dung-heap, which someone's dropped near the barracks. Don't ask me what it's doing there. Perhaps Isarn has cleaned out Berengar's room, at long last. Or perhaps Lord Galhard has decided to redecorate the hall.

The stable boy scampers over to take Esclaramonde's horses, grabbing the reins from her hands. She's looking rather wan, and even more delicate than usual: her enormous eyes are heavy and red-rimmed, with bluish smudges underneath. But she smiles a feeble smile as she looks up and sees Roland.

"My lord," she mutters, "I hope you're well."

"What is it?" he says. "What's wrong?" And he puts out a hand to help her climb down. But she doesn't need any help, slipping to the ground unaided.

"Bad news," she replies. "Good day, Master Pagan."

"Good day, Mistress Maury."

"Why did you come alone?" Roland asks. "Where are the others? What happened?"

"They're not well. We had—we had a shock, this morning." She looks around the bailey with haunted eyes, her fingers locked together so tightly that white patches form on her knuckles. "It's Aribert. He—he—"

Suddenly she puts her clasped hands over her mouth. This is no good. We can't do this here.

"Perhaps we'd better take her inside, my lord."

"Yes," Roland agrees. "Yes, come inside, Mistress. Refresh yourself, and then we can talk."

"He was in a tree." The words burst out of her like spray through a blowhole. "Estolt found him. Hanging there near the farm, with his—with his stomach . . . all cut . . ."

God preserve us. Glance at Roland, who's frozen in midstep.

"There were crows, my lord, they were— they—"

"I understand," he says quietly. "You don't have to explain. Come inside now."

"Yes. Yes, I must speak to Lord Galhard." Her voice steadies; she straightens her shoulders. "I must tell him that it's finished. It's all got to finish. Aribert is dead. Garnier is dead. We must stop it now, before it goes any further." She looks up at Roland. "We must stop it."

A long pause. Finally he touches her arm. "Yes," he says. "Come, we'll talk to Lord Galhard."

Galhard. Where's Galhard? I haven't seen him since yesterday's unpleasant little episode, when we arrived back at the castle. Cornered in bed, under a monstrous, snoring lymer hound, he was complaining of toothache. Rampant black hair all over his chest (in fact you couldn't see where the beard ended and the chest began). Irritable. Dangerous. A poultice jammed in one cheek, muffling his formidable voice. "Dead, eh? Well, I can't say I'm sorry. Must have been brigands. They're always bad in the spring."

"It was you!" Roland cried. "You sent a squad

after them!" Whereupon Galhard glared at us with one bloodshot eye over a tangle of furs and blankets and reeking dog.

"Prove it," he snarled.

Could he still be in bed?

The rushes in the hall feel squishy underfoot, like little dead animals, or the kind of thing that comes out of a horse's rear end. (If someone doesn't get rid of these rushes very soon, they'll be getting up and walking out the door by themselves.) Berengar's throwing dice with Aimery and Isarn, whose face still looks like the ruins of Baalbek. They raise their eyes as we enter.

"What's up?" says Berengar, catching sight of Esclaramonde. "More trouble?" He sounds as if he's been praying for it.

"Where is Lord Galhard?" Roland demands. His gaze freezes on Aimery, who begins to shift about on his bench. (That look is one of Roland's most deadly weapons.) "We must speak to him immediately."

Berengar jerks a thumb at the door behind the dais. "He's still in bed. His tooth's worse. I told him he's going to have to get it pulled."

Roland turns to Esclaramonde. "Sit down," he says. "I'll go and speak to him."

"Can't I speak to him myself?"

"Perhaps. I'll ask. Wait here. You too, Pagan."

He disappears into Galhard's sleeping chamber, and silence descends. Berengar's squinting at Esclaramonde over the rim of his goblet. Aimery's fiddling with the dice. I don't know what Isarn's doing, because I don't want to look.

"What happened to your face, Master Pagan?" Esclaramonde inquires. God help us. Exactly the question I was hoping not to hear.

"Nothing." (Don't look at Isarn, please; just don't look.) "It was an accident."

"Is it painful?"

"A bit."

"What have you been using on it?"

"Oh, nothing."

"No comfrey? Wormwood? Marjoram?"

"N-no."

"Basil is good for headaches. And balm, of course. Chervil will ease the swelling. Perhaps I could make you an infusion." She looks over to where Isarn is skulking, and offers him her sweet, tentative smile. "Both of you."

Isarn grunts, as Berengar slams down his goblet and wipes his mouth.

"Are you an herb-woman?" He leers, displaying the broken remnants of what must have once been a proud wall of teeth. (That mouth's been under siege too often.)

"I care for the sick," Esclaramonde replies coolly. "I live with some people who need a good deal of care."

"Know anything about love philters?"

Groan. But Esclaramonde doesn't even twitch an eyebrow.

"No, my lord," she rejoins. "I've never had any need of them."

Hooray! Roland's back. That was fast. He moves toward us, alert behind a stony expression. The tightness in his shoulders gives him away.

"Lord Galhard will be out shortly," he declares. "Isarn, will you fetch Mistress Maury some food and drink?"

"Isarn's playing dice," Berengar growls. Whoops! Bad tactic. Roland swallows and shifts his chilling stare to Aimery. No argument from that quarter. Aimery slouches off without a single protest. (Probably glad to escape.)

"Did you tell him?" says Esclaramonde, as Roland lowers himself onto a bench. "About Aribert?"

"Yes."

"What did he say, my lord?"

"He said he'd be out shortly."

"Oh."

"Who's Aribert?" Berengar asks. But no one answers. Roland is watching Esclaramonde, who seems to be lost in thought. Isarn's studying the impressive collection of smears and splats and smudges on the tabletop. As for me, I'm keeping my head down.

Suddenly Germain appears, panting.

"My lord?" he says. "Oh, Lord Roland—"

"What is it?" (Berengar.)

"It's the baker, my lord. He just told me—"

"What? Spit it out!"

"They wouldn't let him use the mill, my lord. The abbey mill, at Roncevaux. He can't grind his corn, and neither can anyone else from Bram. Which means they can't bake their bread."

God preserve us. So the Abbot's done it, then. Roland lets out a faint sigh. Berengar's fist hits the table so hard that the floor shakes. But before he can speak, Galhard's voice forestalls him.

"Have they closed the mill?" he mumbles through a mouthful of poultice. He's standing at

213

the door to his chamber, all wrapped up in a fur-lined cloak. Germain jumps and wipes his sweaty forehead.

"Only—only to people from Bram, my lord," he quavers.

"My lord." Roland rises to his feet. "Let me take this to the Templars. It's gone far enough."

"No."

"My lord, I know you haven't paid their peace tax lately, but I'm sure we can work something out—"

"I'll take care of it myself, Roland."

A "hear, hear" from Berengar. He's on his feet, too, and clasping his sword hilt. "If we can't use their damned mill, then we should burn it down!" he roars.

"No!" It's Esclaramonde. She has that look on her face. "My lord, this is senseless. Violence will only beget violence, and God commanded us to love our neighbors as we love ourselves. This is the Devil's work, my lord. God has not given us the spirit of fear, but of power, and of love, and of a sound mind!"

"The Abbot is a neighbor I can do without," Galhard rejoins, and turns to Roland. "Get rid of her," he says.

But Esclaramonde won't be silenced. She steps forward, her dark eyes blazing.

"Why do you judge your brother?" she cries. "We shall all stand before Christ's judgment seat, my lord. We should not judge but love one another, because the fruit of the Holy Spirit is love, and joy, and peace, and gentleness. When Christ was reviled, He didn't revile again. When He suffered, He didn't threaten, but committed Himself to God, who judges with righteousness."

"Get her out of here!" Galhard bawls. Roland, however, doesn't move a muscle.

"What this lady says is the truth, my lord," he responds quietly. "You should listen to her."

"Love your enemies!" (Esclaramonde spreads her hands in a gesture of supplication.) "Do good to them that hate you, my lord. Bless them that curse you, and pray for them who spitefully use you. Let the peace of God rule in your heart, and you will walk as a child of light. For the man who says he is in the light, and hates his brother, is in the most profound darkness. He walks in darkness and knows not where he goes, because the darkness has blinded his eyes. Do not blind yourself, my lord. Lift your eyes to the light."

God, she's magnificent. I've never heard anyone

preach like her. The way she talks is just unbeat-
able. Galhard obviously thinks so, too.

"Shut up!" he thunders. "Get her out of here, or
she'll suffer for it, I promise you!"

But Roland has already taken up a defensive position beside her. If anyone attacks Esclaramonde,
they'll have Roland to deal with as well. "My lord,"
he declares, "what you do now may affect hun-
dreds of people for many years to come. Won't
you reconsider?"

"No!"

"Then I must take this matter to the Templars at
Carcassonne."

"Good! Off you go, then! And I hope you stay
there!" Galhard waves a curt dismissal. "You can
take her with you, while you're at it. I don't want to
see her here again."

"You won't, my lord, but just remember this."
Esclaramonde's voice rings out bravely. "By doing
violence to your brother, you do violence to yourself. If he is wounded, you will bleed. Because he
that doesn't love his brother abides in death, and
whoever hates his brother is a murderer, and no
murderer shall have eternal life. God is love, and
he that dwells in love dwells in God."

Amen. Roland places a hand under her elbow

216

and glances at me. (Out of here, Pagan, before Galhard disembowels someone.) Making a quick but dignified exit.

"Would your community object to providing Pagan and myself with a place to sleep, Mistress Maury?" Roland suddenly inquires as we stagger down the stairs. She looks up at him, startled.

"No, of course not. Why?"

"Then we shall escort you home. You should not be traveling by yourself."

"But—"

"It will only be for one night. Tomorrow we shall start for Carcassonne. I intend to speak to the Temple Commander there."

Esclaramonde stops abruptly and turns to face him.

"You wish to prevent this," she observes. "You wish to discuss a peaceful settlement."

"Yes."

"I honor you, my lord. You are a man of light." And she smiles, almost fiercely. "The Holy Spirit abides in you, because you are one of God's chosen."

Hear, hear, I'll second that. A slow flush creeps across Roland's face.

But he doesn't say a word.

✠CHAPTER EIGHTEEN✠

Mmmmm. That wonderful smell of Templars. That smell of lye and soda and strewing herbs and boiled clothes, so fresh and clear and clean. Not a single dog turd anywhere. Not a whiff of urine. I'd almost forgotten what cleanliness looked like. Nothing but scrubbed stone floors and cobweb-free corners as far as the eye can see.

Of course, the Templars themselves don't smell quite so attractive. They're not supposed to. ("If we were meant to smell like lilies," Sergeant Tibald used to say, "God would have turned the Saracens into bees.") Most Templars announce themselves with a blast of virile aromas—horse, sweat, smoke, garlic, leather—depending on what they've been doing. Commander Folcrand, however, doesn't seem to have been doing very much. Not physically, at least. He exudes a smell of vellum and hot wax, like a notary, and his office is piled high with rolls of parchment. As for that chaplain with the bleached face and inky hands, he looks like a permanent fixture.

"Ah, Brother Roland." Folcrand's voice is gruff and weary. "Welcome back. You've spoken to Lord Galhard?"

"Yes, Commander, but—"

"Sit down, please. And your squire also. Just push those books off that chair; I apologize for the confusion." He grasps the bridge of his nose between his thumb and forefinger, rubbing the corners of his closed eyes. You could hide a leg of mutton in the bags underneath them. His thick, wavy gray hair is all rumpled and ink-stained, as if he's been running frantic hands through it. "We're expecting a visit from the Grand Preceptor, and I'm afraid there seems to be a problem with the accounts. Nothing serious. But it's not easy untangling all these tithes and taxes."

Well, well, will you look at that? Never thought I'd see a nervous Templar. He's got that withdrawn, worried air of someone trying to add up a set of numbers, over and over again, in his head.

Roland decides to skip the courtesies and get down to business.

"Commander Folcrand," he says, "I fear that my errand was unsuccessful. None of my family responded to the appeal for holy warriors."

"Oh." Folcrand fiddles with a quill on the table in front of him. He's obviously dying to get back to his account books. It's strange; he's got the shoulders of an ox and a face like a gravel pit, but he's been completely unmanned by a handful of debts and disbursements. "Well," he remarks, "I can't say I'm surprised. Most of the families in this part of the world won't risk leaving their lands. Things are too unstable."

"Yes." Roland leans forward. "And that's what I wanted to talk about. You see, my father . . . there's trouble brewing between my father and the Abbey of Saint Jerome."

Folcrand grunts. "Wouldn't be the first time," he says.

"No, of course. But in this case my father was not the original culprit." Slowly, solemnly, Roland begins to describe the whole messy business from beginning to end. Garnier. Aribert. Guibert. The ambush on the road. Esclaramonde's gruesome discovery. Over by the window, the chaplain listens with downcast eyes, picking at his fingernails. Sounds of commerce drift up from the street, peddlers' cries and the rumble of wheelbarrows mingling with someone's excruciating rendition of "I Hope I May Lie in a Tavern When Dying." It's nice to hear noises like that. Reminds me of Jerusalem. After so long at Bram, Carcassonne feels like the center of the world.

"And now he is threatening to burn down the mill at Roncevaux," Roland continues. "I very much fear the consequences of such an action, for Bram isn't the only village that relies on the abbey mill. Who will have meal to make bread, in that region, if the mill is destroyed?"

"Hmmph."

"And as you know, the lords of Montferrand have jurisdiction over Saint Jerome. Destroying the abbey mill would be a direct insult to them. Fortunately, it appears that they are not residing at home just now. I believe they're off defending Toulouse from the Count of Poitou—"

"Oh, no, they're not." Folcrand looks up from his goose quill. "Haven't you heard? Richard's withdrawn."

Well, I'll be spit-roasted. This is interesting. Roland, caught off-guard, simply stares.

"King Philip raised an army and attacked Richard's lands in Berry," Folcrand explains. "He captured Châteauroux at the beginning of last week. That's meant a change of plans on Richard's part. He's pulling out of Quercy as fast as he can. So I doubt that the lords of Montferrand will be in Toulouse for much longer."

"I don't understand." Roland sounds dazed. "King Philip—?"

"Raymond of Toulouse is King Philip's vassal. Philip doesn't take kindly to having his authority challenged." Folcrand permits himself a humorless little smile. "Quite apart from the temptation of unprotected territory."

"But King Philip made a vow to join the Crusade!" Roland protests. "So did Richard. They were going to march together. How can they become involved in a petty dispute like this?"

"I know. It's a mess."

"But we were going to march with them!"

Yes, now that's the important point. We were going to march with them. With King Philip, to be precise. We came here to persuade Roland's family that they should join King Philip's crusading force. So what's going to happen to us if that force disappears?

And what's going to happen to Jerusalem?

"Well, don't hold your breath." Folcrand sighs. "We received word from our sister house in London today. It's possible that King Henry of England might come to Richard's rescue and attack Philip himself. If that happens, I can guarantee we won't see any Crusade for at least a year. These cross-channel conflicts always drag on and on."

God preserve us. A year! It's already been that long since the Battle of Hattin. What happened to all those promises? I thought we'd be back in Jerusalem by the end of this summer!

Glancing at Roland, whose face is unreadable.

"In any event," Folcrand concludes, "the point I'm making is that the lords of Montferrand are probably on their way home as we speak."

"Then the outlook is even more serious," says Roland earnestly. "As you know, the abbey owes Roquefire de Montferrand certain rights of jurisdiction. If something isn't done, he and my father will be at each other's throats before the end of the month."

Suddenly there's a knock on the door. "Come in!" Folcrand exclaims. A head like a giant root vegetable makes its appearance.

"Yes, Sergeant?"

"Inventory's finished, my lord."

"Good."

"There seems to be a bit of a mix-up with the bedding—"

"We'll talk about it later."

"Yes, my lord."

The head disappears again. After a brief silence, Folcrand continues.

"As if I didn't have anything else to do but worry about kitchen supplies and loan guarantees," he complains. "Now, where were we? Oh, yes, your father. I'm sorry, Brother Roland, but I don't quite understand what you want."

"Commander, I've been told that in this country the Order has a peacekeeping role, guaranteed at the payment of a peace levy." Roland speaks slowly and carefully, weighing every word. "Your help in this matter may well put a stop to serious conflict. I have come here to ask for that help."

Folcrand drags a hand over the loose skin of his face. Briefly, the crags and furrows rearrange themselves. "The thing is, Brother, it doesn't quite work like that," he confesses. "About forty years ago, the Count of Toulouse, the Viscount of Carcassonne, and the Archbishop of Narbonne established a peace and truce for all peasants, oxen, and other farm animals. The Templars were to receive one setier of grain a year for each plow, in payment, and it was to be collected by the civil authorities. But that wasn't designed to pay for our services so much as to indemnify people in case of theft or destruction. Naturally, with our financial expertise, we were asked to take charge of the levy's overall management."

Financial expertise? What financial expertise? I thought that your account books were ruining your life.

"Of course, we try to play our part in stamping out brigandage," Folcrand continues. "And we advise the Viscount of Carcassonne on major strategic decisions. But as for private disputes between local lords, well, we hardly have the right (or, I may say, the resources) to interfere where we're not welcome. It's not our role to go to war with every minor peer who decides to steal his neighbor's goats. Not for one setier of grain per plow per year."

Well, how much do you want, then? A mill? A castle? A right-of-way with toll privileges? What's happened to this Order? The pilgrims never used to pay us, in Jerusalem.

Glance at Roland. Still not a trace of expression on his face. "What do you want me to do, exactly?"

Folcrand finishes. "Send a fighting force over to Bram, and threaten your father with a siege if he doesn't stop bickering? It can't be done, Brother."

But Roland shakes his head.

"There's no need to use force," he replies. "That will simply aggravate the problem. Disputes like this should be settled by negotiation." He straightens, and places an open hand on his chest. "I cannot act as intermediary. Why should Abbot Tosetus trust the son of Lord Galhard? What we need is a neutral party who won't be affected by the outcome. Someone who would command respect. Someone who is accustomed to dealing with such delicate matters."

"And you think one of my knights would fill that role?"

"Yes, I do."

Folcrand sighs. He frowns down at his hands, which bear the scars of many battles. A bell tolls in the distance. You can hear the brisk sound of footsteps in the corridor outside. "I suppose it's not out of the question," he mutters, and thinks hard. "Brother Ferry may be the man. Ferry de Lezinnes. He's just come back from Lombardy. Things are very unsettled over there." (Turning to the chaplain.) "Go and tell Brother Ferry that I want to see him, will you, Father? He should be on his way to Vespers."

The chaplain bows and scurries off. There's a general sense of movement—of footsteps and slamming doors and hushed voices—as the knights of the house are summoned to prayer.

"I daresay you'll want to attend Vespers yourself, Brother Roland," Folcrand remarks, and it's suddenly quite obvious that he wants to break the news to Lord Ferry himself, in private. Roland instantly shoots to his feet. "Of course," he says. "It would be a privilege."

"Come back after prayers and we'll discuss this further. I'm sure Brother Ferry will be amenable."

"Thank you, Commander."

"No, no, don't thank me."

We're out the door so fast that there's hardly time to draw breath. The corridor seems to be full of large, brown sergeants tottering under great loads of gridirons and saddle covers and dusty old corselets made of horn and boiled leather. (Inventory business?) A bald knight strides past, at top speed, without sparing us a glance. Everyone's busy. Buzz, buzz, buzz.

"I must go to the chapel," Roland observes. "Can you keep yourself occupied until after Vespers?"

"Yes, my lord."

"Meet me back here when the bell rings. You can find your way, can't you?"

"My lord—"

"What?" Looking down his long nose. It's impossible to tell what he's thinking: he's wearing that Man of Marble mask again. Funny how it disappeared for a while at Bram.

"My lord, what about the Crusade? What are we going to do? If King Philip gets involved in a local fight—"

"It may resolve itself quickly."

"But if it doesn't?" (We're not going to war against England, are we? I don't fancy that at all. I want to go back to Jerusalem.) "Surely there are others we could join, instead? What about Emperor Frederick? *He's* taken a vow."

"Later, Pagan, we'll discuss it later."

"But we will return to Jerusalem, won't we? We're not going to stay here?" Catching his arm. Look at me, Roland! This is important! We've got to do something. It's my homeland we're talking about! "What happens if there isn't a Crusade? Will we go back to help Lord Conrad, in Tyre? He needs us more than King Philip does. We can't stay here, my lord. We just can't."

"Pagan," says Roland, and removes my hand from his elbow. "I am a knight of the Temple, sworn to fight for Christ. Why should I stay here and become involved in a war that isn't holy? A Templar knight doesn't draw his sword against Christians. A Templar knight must only shed the blood of Infidels. You know that. So what else could I possibly do?"

"Yes, but things are different now." Casting a glance down the corridor, toward the backs of the equipment-toting sergeants. "This Order is changing. Nobody seems to be worrying about Saladin. Everyone's too busy with Frankish politics."

"Hush! Quiet. Not so loud."

"But it's true!"

"Pagan." His voice is stern. "You don't know what you're talking about. You are clever beyond your years, but you're not qualified to speak of this Order. The blessed Bernard himself said that the knights of the Temple were chosen specifically to guard the tomb that is the bed of the true Solomon. He told us to go forth and repel the foes of the Cross of Christ. That is the foundation of our Rule. Nothing has changed it, and nothing ever will. Now go and help in the stables. I have prayers to attend."

Watching his white linen back as he marches toward the sound of the second bell. Oh, Roland, you're so innocent. Don't you know that everything changes? How can you possibly believe that anything on this earth will always be the same?

Except, perhaps, for the futile squabbling. It seems to me that the squabbling will never end.

‡CHAPTER NINETEEN‡

Here we are at last. Never thought I'd be so happy to see Bram. But even Bram looks good after an entire day on horseback, with Ferry de Lezinnes blabbing away on one side, and Den the Wag— Den the Wit—blocking my view on the other. I suppose there's one thing you can say about Den: at least he makes an effective shield. I mean, what else can you say? He's big. He's there. He's got a lot of hair coming out of both nostrils. That's about it, really.

But it may not be his fault. I'd probably lose the power of speech myself, if I were Lord Ferry's squire. That man just never stops talking. You wonder when he finds the time to breathe, let alone eat or sleep or empty his bladder. It's been yak, yak, yak, ever since we crawled into our saddles at sunrise. And he still hasn't stopped!

"The city was being defended by Lady Carcas, widow of the previous Saracen governor. After a siege of five years, Carcas ordered that the last pig be fed a sack of grain and thrown over the battlements. It burst, of course, and Charlemagne decided that people who fed grain to their pigs would never be starved out. He was just about to withdraw when the trumpet sounded for a parley. The cry went up: 'Carcas sonne!' Which is how the city got its name."

Yak, yak, yak, in that syrupy, singsong accent, which must be northern, I suppose, like the copper curls and the curious design on his scabbard. No wonder Commander Folcrand decided to send him with us. Probably couldn't wait to get rid of him. Clattering across the bridge toward the castle. Its massive sandstone walls gleam like gold in the late afternoon light. Its colors flap sluggishly above the keep, like a couple of dirty old stockings.

"Of course, Charlemagne married Carcas to Trencavel, the bravest of his knights, and gave him the city as a wedding present. It's been in the family ever since."

Yak, yak, yak. (He just goes on and on and on, like the Book of Numbers.) Wait a moment, this is very strange. Why would Isoard be on guard duty? Don't tell me he's joined the garrison? I thought he was a servant. He comes to attention as we pass, his gigantic skull much too big for the borrowed helmet he's wearing.

I wonder if Roland noticed. Probably not. No doubt his senses have been dulled by the ceaseless pounding of Ferry's indomitable voice.

"You're very lucky to share the name of Charlemagne's most illustrious knight, Brother. Probably the greatest of all knights, don't you think? I have to confess, I've always tried to model myself on Roland."

Through the gates and into the bailey. It seems very quiet. Full of dung and straw and long shadows, but nothing much else. One of the stable boys seems to be torturing a small animal near the kitchen. He sees us and scrambles to his feet.

Smoke drifts across the empty expanse of cobbles.

"These fortifications are well constructed," Ferry remarks, "but they don't seem to be properly manned. Is it your father's usual custom to mount a skeleton watch? It seems rather imprudent."

Roland, however, doesn't reply: he's already dismounting, his movements quick and tense. "Germain?" he calls. "Joris? You, boy, where's Germain? Is my father home?"

The stable boy just stares with his slit eyes, an evil grin cracking the dried mud on his face. That little tick wants a good kick up the crupper. I'll do it myself, as soon as I have the time.

Suddenly Bernard appears at the kitchen door, wiping his hands on a towel. He smells of onions.

"Bernard," says Roland, "is my father home?"

A shake of the head. Uh-oh. This doesn't look promising.

"Where is he?"

Bernard would prefer not to say. He scratches his belly. He scratches his chin. His jowls tremble as he wriggles like a worm on a fish hook.

"I don't know, it's not my place," he squeaks. "You must ask Germain."

"Germain's here?"

Bernard points toward the keep. And there's Germain, standing at the top of the stairs. He must have heard Roland shouting.

Even as we turn, he vanishes inside again.

"Who is Germain?" Ferry asks. He's on his feet now, like the rest of us. Doesn't seem overenthusiastic about yielding his horse to that nasty little toad of a stable boy, but doesn't really have any choice. Roland heads straight for the keep, frowning.

You'd swear he'd gone deaf.

"Brother?" Ferry cries. "Brother Roland! Who is Germain?"

"Germain is Lord Galhard's steward." (I suppose someone had better answer the poor fool.) "He's called Germain Bonace."

"Oh, I see. So he's not one of the sons of the house?"

"No, my lord. Lord Galhard's sons are Lord Berengar and Lord Jordan."

"I'm afraid I'm not as well acquainted with the inhabitants of this area as I should be. Of course, I haven't been stationed at Carcassonne very long. And I've met some of the local lords, such as the lords of Pennautier, Bertrand and Aimery-Olivier de Saissac, Raymond de Vintron. . . ."

Yak, yak, yak. Following in Roland's wake, with Den bringing up the rear. Plunging into the dimness of the great hall, which smells like ferrets. Still haven't swept out the rushes, I see. Germain's standing just inside the door, fiddling with his thumb ring: Ademar's draped across a nearby bench, talking to Tayssiras. Why in God's name does she bother with him? He's nearly as old as Germain, and he's also the biggest bore in Languedoc. Thinks he's so superior. So sophisticated. I've *sat* on more sophisticated things than Ademar in my time. And cleaned them up, too.

"Germain," says Roland. "Where is Lord Galhard?"

"My lord—" Germain glances nervously at Ademar, who slowly rises. I hate the way Ademar sucks his cheeks in like that. Does he think it makes him look serious? Important? What a laugh.

"My lord," he says, "events have escalated considerably since you were last in residence." (Groan. Just listen to the way he talks!) "As a result of unprovoked aggression, Lord Galhard has been obliged to undertake several excursions into the territories of Abbot Tosetus."

"What do you mean?" Roland speaks sharply, and Germain flinches. "He didn't burn down the mill, did he?"

"Yes, my lord." (Ademar.) "On the very day you left."

"After which the Abbot's men came in stealth," Germain adds nervously, "and pulled up the vines in the vineyard of Saint Felix, and burned them."

"So Lord Galhard, who was naturally enraged,

236

took an armed force to the abbey," Ademar concludes. "With Lord Jordan and Lord Berengar."

Dead silence. Suddenly Roland looks a good deal older. Ferry shakes his head. Den spits. (It's his only form of communication.)

"When did they leave?" Roland asks in a hoarse voice.

"This morning, my lord, just before sunrise."

"Then they'll be there already. . . ."

God preserve us. I knew this would happen. And it's going to keep on happening, too. What can a blowhole like Ferry do to stop it? These people were bred to fight.

There's a glum kind of pause as the news sinks in. Germain shuffles uneasily. Tayssiras fingers the pendant on her bosom. Den shifts his weight from his right foot to his left.

"It was his toothache, my lord," Germain says at last. "Lord Galhard said he needed to do something to take his mind off his toothache. It was very bad."

"How many people were killed?"

"My lord?"

"How many people were killed?" You can see the sweat gleaming on Roland's face. "At Roncevaux? How many?"

"I don't know, my lord."

"Should we follow Lord Galhard to the abbey, Brother?" Ferry interrupts. "Or should we wait until he returns? How far is the abbey from here?"

"About half a day's ride."

"Then it's too late to set out. We'd be foolish to start now, even if we did go." Ferry sounds brisk and unperturbed. "I suggest that we eat and sleep, and if they aren't back by noon tomorrow, we should go after them."

Hear, hear. No more riding, not tonight. My backside's completely worn away. My spine feels as if it's been stewed. My eyeballs are still bouncing.

Roland sits down abruptly, as if he's gone weak at the knees.

"No," he murmurs, "we must leave as soon as possible."

"But not now, Brother. That would be foolish. That would be dangerous."

"Please, my lord." (Have some mercy. I'm falling to pieces here.) "Please, my lord, couldn't we rest? Think of the horses."

Roland looks at me with glazed eyes. This blow has hit him hard. Very, very hard.

"We shall leave at first light," Ferry declares, and turns to Germain. "I am Lord Ferry de Lezinnes, of the Knights Templar. This is my squire, Den. We require some food and two beds, as soon as possible."

"Y-yes, my lord."

"You can put us in here, if you like. Whatever's most convenient. Den will help you."

All of a sudden, everybody's moving. Ademar disappears. Tayssiras slips out. Roland stands up, grabs a candle, and heads for the circular staircase. Clump, clump, clump. His footfalls are heavy and hopeless.

Ferry calls after him: "Where are you going, Brother?"

"To pray."

"Good idea. I'll join you presently."

God preserve us. Can you imagine? I foresee the world's longest prayer. Roland's still climbing: clump, clump, clump. I suppose he's off to the chapel.

"My lord?"

He doesn't seem to hear me. Following his footsteps up the staircase, into Berengar's room. It's empty, of course, except for the dogs.

"My lord? Wait."

He stops. Turns. His face is white and heavy; his shoulders droop. Poor Roland.

"My lord, it's not your fault. There's nothing we could have done. You're not responsible for your family."

How many times do I have to say it? But it bounces straight off him like an arrow bouncing off a battlement. He just sighs.

"My lord, they don't care about you. Why worry about them?"

"I know you're right, Pagan." His voice is low and unsteady. "In my head I know you're right, but not in my heart."

And off he goes to the chapel. Should I go with him? Probably not. Crossing the next threshold, taking a deep breath, and *phew!* What's that smell? It smells like urine! Who's been pissing in our room?

Oh, for—this is disgusting. Disgusting! Where—? My bed. It's coming from my bed.

Someone's been pissing on my palliasse.

Isarn. It must have been Isarn. Or Isoard? No, I don't think Isoard's even allowed up here. Anyway, Isoard didn't get his skull bashed in. It's got to be Isarn.

That stinking, pestiferous pus-bag.

I'm going to kill that reptile.

No, I'm not. Calm down, Pagan. Take a deep breath; think carefully. What can you do? There must be something you can do. Piss on *his* bed? No, that would be stupid, because you're going to be using his bed tonight. You're not going to sleep in a puddle of piss.

What, then? Come on, Pagan, use your brain.

Stumbling back into Berengar's room. There's Isarn's palliasse, with his possessions stacked neatly around it. His best pair of boots; his hunting horn; his festival surcoat. I wonder . . .

No. On second thought, I won't relieve myself all over them. Somehow that wouldn't be—I don't know. Why stoop to his level? Besides, Roland wouldn't like it. He wouldn't like it at all.

I know what I'll do. I'll hide them. I'll stash them away somewhere. But where? The stables? He's always in there. And the barracks are always crawling with people. So is the kitchen. The chapel? Too empty . . .

The cellars. That's it, the cellars.

Putting down my lamp. Dumping everything onto Isarn's blanket: tying the corners together, and slinging the whole lot over my shoulder. Picking up the lamp again. Can't hear anyone on the stairs. If I'm asked, I'll say that this is a bag of dirty laundry. And what will I do with my palliasse? Can't just leave it there: a smell like that will kill

Roland, if he has to breathe it in all night. I suppose I'll have to drag it into the bailey and let it soak up a bit of rain.

Down, down, down, past the great hall. The stairs get clammier and more slippery. Careful, Pagan, you don't want to break your neck. Reaching level ground, at last. God, but it's dark down here: dark and cold. The hollow tinkle of water dripping, somewhere nearby.

Taking it slowly, step by step, through the first big room. Shadows dancing in the flickering light of my lamp. Iron rings thrust high into the walls. (What for? I wonder.) Pikes and rusty axes. A knot of rope. There's that milk churn again.

Now, where should I hide this bag? Inside a cask? Behind that cluster of old trestles?

Suddenly, a noise. A rat? No, rats don't squeal like that. A pig? A puppy?

A person?

"Who's there?" No answer. Don't tell me Galhard's got someone else imprisoned down here. My heart's pumping so hard that the flame on my lamp quivers with every beat.

"I heard you! Who is it? You might as well come out."

Taking a few steps forward. There! A rustle. A movement. (I wish I had my sword.) Swinging the bag in one hand, just in case somebody springs. If you do, my friend, you'll get a faceful of Isarn's best boots. Pushing my lamp into one shadowy corner . . .

And it's Ademar, blinking up at me. Hair ruffled. Knees bare. Tunic flapping.

Beside him, Tayssiras.

"What are you doing here? You're not allowed down here!" He's blustering, panting, sweating. And she—she just sits there, with hardly anything on.

"If you say one word about this, I'll slit you open!" Ademar spits, rising to his feet. She stays where she is, but her hand moves. Slowly, smoothly, she brushes a lock of hair from her impassive face.

Shameless. She's shameless. How could she ever—she's just—and with *him*?!

"Did you hear me?" he croaks. "I mean it! I'll kill you—"

Whump! Throw the bag. It hits him right in the chest, and he reels back, falling. Turn and run. Run. I've got to get out. I can't breathe down here.

It's like a sewer! Writhing around in the muck, like a pair of maggots, like rutting pigs, it makes me sick. I'm going to be sick! Oh, Jesus.

This place, this place, this filthy place. This place is the Devil's work.

‡CHAPTER TWENTY‡

You can't really blame her, I suppose.

After all, Germain's an old man. As for most of the other people at Bram, well, you only have to listen to Berengar. He's so crude and filthy. At least Ademar doesn't have a foul mouth. At least he talks about love and courtship and nightingales, instead of teats and rumps and wantons. Fancies himself as a bit of a courtly lover, I suspect. Makes him look superior. I've even heard him quoting poetry, in his arguments with the other guards. Talking about Twin Souls and the Garden of Happiness and the Triumph of Love over Intellect. I mean, you can't blame her for being swept off her feet.

And of course, lots of women do that kind of thing, especially in the summertime. Even married ones. Even queens. You only have to listen to the troubadours' songs. Some women can't help it: they're like flowers, giving off a beautiful perfume. They just can't help attracting bees.

"*Pagan.*"

(Whoops!) "Yes, my lord?"

"What's the matter with you?" Roland, up ahead, craning around to see what I'm doing. "Wake up, Pagan. This is no time for daydreaming. Can't you see we've arrived?"

So we have. I didn't even notice the vineyards. And there are the abbey walls, with those square church towers rising above them, and a few stray sheep wandering through the ancient, overgrown rubble that lies half-buried not far from the gates. (Ruins of an old guest house? Or barn? Or chapel?) Wisps of smoke dissolve into the air. A perfectly good leather bucket lies on the road in a mess of squashed vegetable peelings.

Ferry frowns when he sees it.

"That doesn't look good," he says. Beside me, Den loosens his sword in its scabbard.

The gates stand open, unmanned. Not a soul to be seen. Entering cautiously, through a terrible absence of noise: no pots clanging, no people talking, just the mournful sound of crows and the ominous hum of flies. Flies everywhere, buzzing and swarming just inside the gates, where a dead servant is sprawled in the dirt. He's still clasping a hoe, his dried blood almost black in the sunlight. May God have mercy. (Turning away.) May God have mercy, what a mess. Ferry crosses himself, but Roland doesn't move a muscle. He seems to have turned to stone.

Pressing on past the trampled gardens, with their broken sticks and flattened shoots, and a scarecrow now wearing rich, embroidered vestments—feastday clothing—all purple and white and crimson. More flies are feeding on a dead pig, which is also wrapped in the remains of a priest's garment, a cope perhaps, but so torn and muddy and soaked in blood that it's impossible to tell. Everywhere the ground is covered in litter: discarded shovels and waterbuckets, bits of clothing, a disemboweled feather pillow, a smashed earthenware bowl, a dead chicken, an uprooted sapling, the ripped and scattered pages of an illuminated book. There's a large barrel standing about fifteen paces from the church's western door. Beside it, a statue of Saint John the Baptist lies broken on the ground, its wreckage still clad in somebody's chain-mail hauberk.

This is unbelievable. I've never seen anything like this. They've been jousting with Saint John the Baptist!

"Den, you stay with the horses," Ferry says quietly as he dismounts. "If anyone bothers you, I give you permission to retire."

Den nods. But what about me? Roland? What should I do? He's already making for the church, both hands on his sword hilt. Well, I'm not staying here with Den. Anything but that. Wait, Roland! Wait for me! Slipping from the saddle. Chasing him up the shallow flight of stairs, past a puddle of vomit, and beneath the carved stone Judgment over the western door. There's a strong smell of wine. Wine and incense and something else. Horses? It can't be.

Advancing into the candle-lit gloom. Whoops! Ferry almost trips over a body, which can't be dead, because it groans and rolls over. Wounded? No, drunk. It's Pons, and he's drunk. The light trickles in through broken windows, splashing onto the tiled floor and painted walls and the columns that stand to attention on both sides of the center aisle, propping up a very lofty, vaulted ceiling.

Crunch, crunch. It's all glass and straw and manure underfoot: horse manure, to be precise. Fresh and steaming. The horses have been stabled along the southern wall, beneath a mural depicting Christ's entry into Jerusalem. The altar has been stripped: no plate, no cloth, no crucifix. A smashed cask has flooded the chancel with wine.

And someone has hacked the Holy Virgin's face off.

"God forgive this desecration," Ferry mutters, with more awe than anger in his voice. Our footsteps echo as we move slowly toward the chancel, between several piles of demolished furniture. There's even a door, pulled right off its hinges. And here's the altar cloth, spread across the floor. Covered in chewed bones and bread crumbs and nutshells. There's also a person, rolled up in a tablecloth, snoring. I can't tell who it is.

"Well, stone me. Look who's here."

A familiar croak. Turn around, and it's Berengar. Leaning against one wall, his legs stretched out in front of him. The right leg is tied up in a blood-stained rag, just above the knee. There's a torn piece of tapestry draped around his shoulders, and his face is the color of tripe.

"One of those damned castrates caught me with

an axe," he says in husky tones. "It didn't do much damage, but it hurt like the devil. Can you find Isarn for me? I need a drink. And a blanket. It's cold in here."

Sounds as if he should be in bed. Ferry glances doubtfully at Roland, who's staring at Berengar with eyes so blank that they could have been painted on.

"It doesn't have to be Isarn," Berengar continues. "It can be anyone. Kick that lazy beggar awake, why don't you? He'll do just as well."

Roland spins on his heel, abruptly, and heads for the door to the cloisters. Obviously wouldn't waste spit on Berengar. We pass from shadows into sunshine, from silence into a babble of voices, and here's the familiar paved courtyard with its little stone seats, every seat fully occupied. There's Isarn, and Aimery, and Joris, and the rest of Galhard's troops. They're lolling about in a rich and dazzling confusion that reminds me of the markets at Acre: a confusion of Damascus rugs, jade inkwells, golden candlesticks, ivory caskets, sandalwood combs, fine linen, amber, alabaster, ebony, amethyst. All mixed up with a less exotic mess consisting mainly of dried fruit, smashed crockery, gardening tools, and a burst flour bag.

"Lord Roland," says Aimery as the laughter leaves his wine-flushed face. They're all drunk and rowdy. Isarn is wearing a monk's habit over his hauberk.

"Where is Lord Galhard?" Ferry demands. "Where is the Abbot? What have you done with the monks?"

Aimery begins to giggle. The others just gape. Roland moves toward the chapter house.

"Where is Lord Galhard?" Ferry repeats angrily. I suppose I'd better follow Roland. This is like a nightmare.

The chapter house smells. It smells of corruption. There's someone sitting on the Abbot's throne, but he's dead. He's been dead a long, long time.

Gagging and choking. I feel sick. Stumbling back out into the cloister garth, into the fresh air, I just can't believe it. They must have dug up a grave. They must have *dug up a grave*, and put the corpse on the Abbot's throne. O God, the heathen are come into thine inheritance; Thy holy temple have they defiled.

"Brother!" Ferry, hailing Roland. "Brother, where are you going? These men know where we can look."

But Roland doesn't seem to hear. Something's

wrong with him: he moves clumsily, as if he's been wounded. Knocking against walls and pillars, grazing his knuckles, stubbing his toes. Lurching through the next door, and the next door, and the next. Going so fast that I have to run to catch up.

Suddenly we're in the refectory. It's a long, narrow room full of tables and benches, with a pulpit at one end and a table on a dais at the other. There's a dead monk near the door. He must have dragged himself all the way from the dais, to judge by the trail of smeared blood. And there, beyond the dead monk, two living ones. Two naked monks, on their hands and knees, with raised marks on their backs and necks and haunches, scrambling over the floor toward a wooden spoon. I know those marks. Those marks are lash marks. They're the marks of the dog whip clasped in Jordan's bloody right hand.

Jordan. He's sitting on one of the tables, stringy-haired, bleary-eyed, wobbling about like a candle flame in a gusty breeze. Slurring his words. "Fetch! Fetch!" as he cracks the whip against a table leg. Severely, profoundly intoxicated.

He doesn't even recognize Roland at first. Just peers at him with bloodshot eyes, brows puckered in perplexity.

Roland advances.

"Oh, no, it's Roland." The truth dawns at last. Light pierces Jordan's alcoholic fog. "Attack! Get him, boys! Get the nasty Templar! Woof, woof!"

He's on his feet as Roland reaches him. I can't see Roland's face, but I can see the muscles knotting under his surcoat as he clenches his fists. *Whump!* He leaps on Jordan, who falls backward, caught by surprise. Roland with a handful of Jordan's collar, slamming him against the tabletop. (*Whomp! Whomp!*) But Jordan's fighting back now, grinding his hand into Roland's face. Bucking against Roland's grip. They roll off the table and crash to the floor.

The monks are moaning and weeping. They huddle there, flinching at the sound of each blow. You idiots! This is your chance!

"Get out!"

They stare at me.

"Get out! Go on! Quick!"

But they're too scared to move. All right, then, be like that. Turning back to the fight, and I can't make out what's going on. It's just a tangle of thrashing limbs. Cries. Thumps. Benches tipping over. All at once Jordan disengages and lurches to his knees. Roland grabs at him, but gets kicked in

253

the chest. Jordan scrambles upright, staggers over to one of the benches and hurls it at Roland, who's coming after him. Roland catches the oak on his hunched shoulder. God! What a clout! He falters, and Jordan takes advantage. Throws a punch, hammering down on Roland's neck. Roland drives his head into Jordan's midriff. They fall again, locked together.

God, God, God, what am I going to do?

That ghastly shouting. Blood on Roland's ear. Blood on his face. Dragging Jordan's arm back, back, back. *"Oof!"* Jordan's knee in Roland's groin. Jordan on his feet again, his mouth a mass of blood, tottering, giddy, groping for his sword. Kicks Roland's ribs. (Groan.) Kicks at his head, but Roland grabs the foot before it makes contact. Dragging his brother down, toppling him, slamming his elbow hard onto Jordan's spine.

"My lord—my lord—"

It's no match, really. Maybe it would be, if Jordan wasn't so drunk. Roland pulls him up and throws him across one of the benches. *Crack!* He slides off facedown and tries to crawl. Roland pulls him up again, by his belt and collar. Throws him against a table. *Crack!* This time he ends up on his side, shielding his face with one arm, groaning, whimpering. Roland seizes a great iron lamp stand (No! No!). Brings it down hard across Jordan's back.

"My lord! Stop! No, my lord, no!"

Roland! In God's name, what are you doing? Grabbing his arm as he raises the lamp stand again. But he's too strong. *Whump!* It slams down on Jordan's pelvis.

"Stop it! Stop it!" (The stand! Grab the stand! Hanging on for dear life.) "No, my lord! No! You'll kill him, you'll kill him!"

Roland strains against my weight. He turns his head slowly, and looks at me with eyes that are totally blank—glazed, unseeing. This isn't Roland. Help. Help! No, Roland, no! It's me!

Breathe again. It's all right. He knows me now. For a moment there I thought that I was dead and buried. But he blinks, and his muscles relax, and he lowers the stand until one end of it touches the floor.

That's it, Roland, take it easy. Calm down. Removing the cold, black shaft from his grip (God, it's heavy) as he moves away, gasping, the blood trickling down his mottled face. He limps over to an upright bench and collapses onto it, his breathing harsh and raw, his movements stiff.

All right, Pagan, first things first. Number one,

restore the lamp stand to its original position. (That's easily done, even though my hands are shaking.) Next, have a look at Jordan. Is he dead? No, he's alive. But he groans softly with each breath (cracked ribs?) and his eyes are closed. Praise God that he wasn't struck on the head. That stand would have fractured his skull.

"Brother Roland?"

It's Ferry, at the door. Oh, go away, please.

"I found Lord Galhard, Brother," Ferry announces. "He seems quite ready to leave. Keeps talking about some kind of marriage negotiations. Apparently the bride-to-be's father is expected at Bram shortly. Lord Galhard wants to be there to welcome him." Ferry crosses the threshold, and pauses. His gaze sweeps the room. "What's going on?" he demands.

"Please, my lord—"

"Brother? What's all this about?"

But Roland doesn't reply. He's sitting at one of the tables, his face hidden in his folded arms.

"Brother!" Ferry's voice is sharp and anxious. "You should talk to Lord Galhard, Brother. He seems to be drunk and he won't tell me where the Abbot is. Most of the monks are locked up in the cellars, but

I can't find the Abbot. We can't settle anything without the Abbot."

"My lord, please. Lord Roland can't talk just now." Go away, I'm begging you. "He needs time to recover."

"What happened?"

"There's been a fight, my lord. Maybe — maybe you could gather everyone together somewhere? Then we can discuss things properly."

You can tell that Ferry doesn't like being told what to do. But he has to admit I've made a sensible suggestion.

"I'll go and fetch Den," he says at last. "We'll tell Lord Galhard's men to report to the church. But I won't release the monks until we find the Abbot, or we may not be able to control them. I just hope the Abbot's not dead." He eyes Roland thoughtfully. "No doubt you'll have recovered by the time I return, Brother. I certainly hope so. Otherwise this is going to be even more difficult than I anticipated."

Yes, that's right, go away. Get lost. Waiting until he's disappeared from sight: turning to Roland — he still hasn't moved — but at least he's breathing. "My lord! My lord, are you hurt? Are you all right? Answer me!"

He raises his head a little. His beard is soaked in blood and sweat. There's a ragged cut extending from the bridge of his nose all the way down to the left side of his jaw. I don't think it's very bad, but I don't like the way he winces when he tries to look around.

"Where does it hurt, my lord? Is anything broken? You should let me check—"

"No," he gasps, "I'm all right. It's nothing."

Nothing? Is that what you call it? Look at you, Roland. Look at what you've done.

"Listen, my lord." Pressing his arm. "You've got to get out of here. You can't stay here." I can feel him trembling: he looks at me sideways. "Please, my lord. Let's leave Languedoc. Let's go now."

Slowly, painfully, he shakes his head.

"My lord, this place is poison! It's poisoning you! You've got to get away, before you lose everything!" (Before I lose you, Roland.) "Please, my lord. I don't understand families; I've never had one. But there's something wrong here. They're like parasites; they're sucking you dry. They're pulling you apart. They're dragging you down, my lord." What is it? What are you shaking your head for? Look around, Roland! Is this the work of a Templar knight? Is this a Holy War? "In God's name, don't

258

shake your head at me! Look at what you've done! You almost killed your own brother! I can't stand it, I just can't. This isn't you. This is them. Please, my lord, please, I won't stand by and let this happen."

"I can't go," he says hoarsely. "Not yet."

"Why? You can't stop this! No one can! Give me one good reason why we should stay!"

"Because there may be more killing." Every word is forced out. "And the innocent must be protected."

"The innocent?" Sweet saints preserve us! "What innocent? Who is innocent, in all of this? Who?"

His eyes are no longer blank and dazed. They're full of feeling. Full of anguish.

"Esclaramonde," he murmurs. "Esclaramonde is innocent."

There's something about a warm, well-watered, flourishing kitchen garden. It makes you think about God. The swelling cucumbers, snuggled in their soft beds of loam; the neat rows of strawberry plants; the almond blossom; the apple trees; the sweet-smelling, flowery borders; the happy hum of bees in the sunlight. It's so peaceful, so healing. And such a beautiful day, despite this morning's horror. Not too hot, not too harsh, with a gentle breeze and a soaring, cloudless sky.

No wonder they're thanking God for it, these women. No wonder they're singing songs of praise. The words of a psalm drift over the seedbeds, high and thin: *"Praise ye Him, all His angels: praise ye Him, all*

His hosts. Praise ye Him, sun and moon praise ye Him, stars of light . . ." And there they are, picking beans. Tall Garsen; fragile Helis; Garnier's daughter Braida, with her disfiguring birthmark and her old green gown. Garnier's widow, sharing a basket with her mother. And Esclaramonde. That must be Esclaramonde in the wide straw hat, with the basket on her arm. She straightens and turns, and—

Yes, that's Esclaramonde. You can see her smile gleaming in the shadow of her hat brim as she jokes with Braida.

Beside me, Roland stops. Is he going to faint? No, he doesn't look too bad. I'm so afraid that he'll just keel over suddenly, without warning. He still limps, and the bruises are beginning to show all over his face and neck and knuckles. Those knuckles! What a mess. So swollen that he could hardly hold the reins in one hand. And I can tell that his guts hurt, too, from the way he breathes. But of course he won't let me help him with anything. He won't even complain. Not a single grunt of protest has passed his lips since we left the abbey.

"My lord? Perhaps you ought to lie down for a while. Perhaps you should rest."

No answer. He seems to be lost in a dream, gazing at the women as they pick and sing and occasionally slap at an insect. They're serene, industrious, intent, like a group of monks at prayer. All at once Esclaramonde looks up and sees us. She stiffens. Gradually the singing falters; the hands freeze; the heads turn.

They're like a herd of grazing animals, sensing the presence of wolves.

Esclaramonde puts her basket down. She moves toward us, a little figure in a big hat, like a mushroom. (How pretty she looks in that ridiculous hat.) As she draws closer, her eyes fall on Roland's wounds, and they widen.

"Lord Roland!" she exclaims. "What happened to you?"

"It's nothing. It's not important."

"But your face! And your fingers—"

"There's been trouble. More trouble." He steps backward, as Esclaramonde reaches for his right hand. "I must talk to you about your safety."

"First let me dress these wounds. They haven't even been cleaned—"

"No, there isn't time."

"What do you mean? Don't be foolish." She sounds almost angry as she grabs his wrist. But her hands are very gentle, feather-light and cautious, examining his swollen fist as if it's an injured duck-

262

ling. "You need care. You're in pain. You're not breathing properly. You should rest."

"That's what I told him. But he won't listen." (You might as well ask a pig to shell peas.) "Please, my lord, Mistress Maury knows all about herbs and healing. Why don't you let her help you?"

He struggles for an answer, flushed and tense, the veins standing out on his forehead. Esclaramonde waves at her companions. It's a wave that means "Keep working."

"I'll be back soon!" she calls, adding quietly, "Somehow I knew that this was too good to last." But the words are barely out of her mouth before she regrets them. She smiles a flustered smile as she turns back to Roland. "I'm sorry, that was discourteous. I don't mean that you're unwelcome. Not at all. It's just that—more bad tidings, on such a beautiful day—but I mustn't keep you standing in this heat. Come, we'll go to the kitchen—"

"Wait." Roland suddenly finds his tongue. His voice is jerky and abrupt. His expression is strained. "There's something I must ask you."

She stares at him in surprise. "Of course," she says.

"It puzzles me—I don't understand—how can you say that this world is the work of the Devil?"

Suddenly Roland seems very young. Younger than Esclaramonde. Younger even than me. "In a garden like this, on a day like this, with all your loving friends and in the midst of such bounty." He gestures at the budding fruit, the blazing flowers. "How can you say that this is the kingdom of darkness? Surely this is a gift from God?"

Hear, hear, that's just what I was thinking. If it's such a beautiful day, how could it possibly be evil? Esclaramonde lowers her gaze, and the brightness, the energy, seems to drain from her face.

"It may be lovely, but it is still the Devil's realm," she murmurs. "It must be so."

"Why? I don't understand why you believe this. Why do you follow such a morbid faith?" Roland's almost pleading now. "There are bad things, I know. There is blood and pain and suffering, but there are good things, too. God's love is all around us."

"No." She's shaking her head. "God has no power in this world."

"But how can you say that?"

"Because it's true! It must be!" She looks up at last, and her eyes are moist and fierce. "I once had a husband," she chokes. "I also had a baby son. A tiny baby, nine weeks old, who died. He died in

264

great pain, great suffering—" She stops for a moment. Swallows. Proceeds. "If God is good, if God is loving, how could He have allowed that to happen? Death comes to us all, but not that kind of suffering. That was the Devil's work. The priest said my baby must have suffered for *my* sins, but I don't believe it. A loving God wouldn't punish an innocent child for the sins of his mother. Only a monster would do such a thing."

God preserve us. More misery. It's all too much. I'm so sick of the endless sorrow and anger and betrayal. When will it end? When are we going to get a bit of peace and quiet?

"So you see," Esclaramonde concludes, in a much softer voice, "though it's very difficult, sometimes, and there are many things that trouble me, I have to believe that this world is the kingdom of darkness. Otherwise, nothing makes sense." A pause as she studies Roland's battered features. "It's the only way I can live, my lord. Do you understand?"

No reply from Roland, whose face has lost all its color. He swallows and bites his lip, but he doesn't say a word. Perhaps he really doesn't understand. I do, though. I understand why she became a heretic, at least in my head. In my heart, however,

265

I just can't believe that this garden is the work of the Devil. I've seen the Devil's work before, several times. And this isn't it.

"Come, my lord." (She's given up waiting for an answer.) "We can't talk here. Let me dress your wounds, and we can sit down and have a drink. Come, you shouldn't be standing on that leg."

She leads us to her dwelling in silence. Past the storehouse. Across the farmyard. Removing her hat at the door. Old Grazide, Garsen's mother, is the only person inside: she's sitting near the hearth, snoring, propped up in a high-backed chair. It's very dim in this room, but you can just make out the table, and the benches, and the entrance to the sleeping chamber. Dirt floor. Oak chests. Firewood. A basket of mushrooms. Esclaramonde speaks softly, so as not to disturb the old woman. "Sit down, my lord. You, too. Master Pagan. There's mead. Would you like some?" Producing the cups that we used last time. Blue glass cups; her very best. "Where are your horses?"

"Othon took them."

"Oh, yes, of course. Is that too strong?" She watches intently as I swallow my first draft. "Do you want some water in it?"

"No, thank you."

"Mistress—" Roland begins, but she darts into the next room, returning with a handful of olive leaves, a mortar, and a pestle.

"Crushed olive leaves are good for cleaning wounds," she explains.

"Mistress—"

"Forgive me, my lord, could you just give me one moment? I want to be sitting down when I hear this."

She bustles about, filling a small iron pot with water from a large bucket, placing the pot on the table, rummaging in one of the oak chests, producing several pieces of clean linen. Finally she sits down next to Roland and starts grinding away at the olive leaves, which fill the air with a fresh, clean smell.

"Now," she observes, "what were you saying?"

"Mistress, I have to tell you that your fears have been realized." Roland uses his crispest, driest, most official Commander-of-the-Temple voice. "After we left for Carcassonne last week, my father took a force and burned down the abbey mill at Roncevaux."

A sigh from Esclaramonde.

"Shortly afterward, the Abbot sent men to burn the vines in one of my father's vineyards. My father responded by desecrating the abbey."

Esclaramonde bites her lip and shakes her head.

"I have also heard," Roland continues, "that the lords of Montferrand may be returning from Toulouse. They have some jurisdiction over the abbey. If they do return, and hear what has happened to it, they will almost certainly want vengeance."

"God forgive them," Esclaramonde groans. "God forgive them all."

"For this reason, your community is no longer safe here," Roland finishes. "You would be much safer if you came to Bram, where it will be easier to protect you."

She looks at him, astonished.

"But we can't go to Bram!" she exclaims.

"You must."

"No." (Shaking her head firmly.) "No, that's not possible. What about Grazide? What about Helis? They are both very frail. Sitting in that bumpy cart would be so bad for them."

"Mistress Maury, I don't think you understand—"

"Besides, why should the lords of Montferrand trouble themselves with us?" Esclaramonde dips

268

her hand into the iron pot, and sprinkles some water on her crushed olive leaves. "We have no quarrel with them. We are harmless. No, my lord, I thank you, but you mustn't worry. I'm sure we'll be quite safe."

"Listen to me!" Roland speaks so sharply that Esclaramonde jumps, and Grazide chokes on a snore. The old woman opens one bleary eye. "This is not a game," he snaps. "This is serious. My father has killed several of the abbey brethren. He took the Abbot, and stripped him, and covered him in honey, and left him outside for the ants and bees, so that by the time we found him he was almost mad. My father dug up the corpse of the former Abbot and placed it in the chapter house. He locked the monks in a cellar with a savage dog. He slaughtered a pig in the crypt, and threw its guts around the nave—"

"Please, my lord." She puts her hands to her ears. "No more, please."

"Do you think that the lords of Montferrand will forgive him for this?" Roland leans toward her. "Will they think: 'Do good to them which hate you'? No. They will think: 'An eye for an eye.' They will want to do the same to my father. But my father will be well armed, and well protected.

269

So instead of attacking him, they will attack his vassals. They will attack farms like this one. The Abbot will tell them, 'Those heretics started all this,' and they will come here because they believe that it's good to kill heretics—"

Roland stops suddenly as Esclaramonde covers her eyes with one hand. He pulls back and glances at me. Don't look like that, Roland; it's the truth. It had to be said. She can't hide from the truth.

But when she unveils her eyes, they're quite tranquil.

"If they come, they come," she says quietly. "I would rather stay and protect our home than run away and leave it. We've weathered other storms. We'll weather this one. There's always the forest to hide in, and I would prefer the forest to your father's protection, Lord Roland. No offense meant."

Mad. She's mad. Does she want to die? Roland watches as she picks up the mortar and begins to grind leaves again, reducing them to a sticky green paste.

"Please," he says at last. His voice is so gentle, so muted, that she can't help glancing up in surprise. "Please, my father has nothing to do with this. I have come here to fulfill a duty of protection. I can't let you stay here. I can't let you run such a risk. Do

270

you think that I can just walk away? If anything happened to you, I would never forgive myself."

Sweet saints preserve us. Sweet saint — could it be? Could it really be? I've never heard him so . . . so . . . if only I could see his face!

But his face is turned to Esclaramonde. They're practically eye to eye. And suddenly she blushes a deep, fiery pink. Blushes and looks down at her hands.

"Please," he murmurs, "if you don't leave, then we must stay."

"Very well." She still won't look at him, but keeps her gaze firmly locked on the paste she's grinding. "If you insist, we'll go to Bram."

"Tomorrow."

"Very well, tomorrow."

Roland sighs. I can't believe it. I just can't believe it. She's a heretic! How could someone like Roland—? But she's very good, of course. Very, very good. And so is he. . . .

Oh, God. And I bet he doesn't even realize. What will happen when he does? It'll never work. It's a disaster, a complete disaster. He'd be better off falling in love with a unicorn. Or a stained-glass window. Or a Turkish princess.

God preserve us. What's going to happen now?

CHAPTER TWENTY-TWO

Ademar is guarding the castle gates. He gawks at the overloaded wagon as it creaks toward him, barely big enough to contain the sixteen blankets, twelve cooking pots, and ten tightly packed bodies that have somehow been squeezed onboard. But he recognizes Esclaramonde, and comes to attention as Roland passes.

So Galhard made it back, then. I wonder how Ferry managed to get him out of the abbey. With a boot up the backside? Looks as if we'll never know, because Galhard certainly won't tell us. As for Ferry, I can guarantee that we won't be seeing him at Bram. If he's not still clearing things up at

Saint Jerome, I suppose he'll be on his way back to Carcassonne by now.

"Stop here," says Roland. He's talking to Estolt, who drags at the reins of his two plodding cart-horses. They come to a halt just inside the gates. "I'm going to talk to my father," Roland continues. "It shouldn't take long. If you would just wait here, I'll be back in a moment." Turning toward the stables. "You! Boy! Take my mare."

And mine too, please. Dismounting more quickly than Roland (for once) beneath the hostile gaze of Isarn, who's hovering near the kitchen. There's Bernard, too. And Pons. In fact the bailey seems to be full of sluggish, aimless people with nothing better to do than stop and stare at our wagonload of unexpected visitors.

"Is Lord Galhard in the keep?" Roland asks Bernard. (He obviously can't bring himself to talk to Isarn.) Bernard nods, and Roland flaps a hand at me. Come on, Pagan.

Moving toward the keep across the greasy, gray cobbles.

That keep. That sink of a keep. Murky and somber in the half-light, streaks of damp on its featureless walls, its crenelated battlements like the jagged ruins of a rotten tooth against the sky. How

I hate it. Woe to the bloody city, to the pot whose scum is therein. Walking through the door of this miserable place is like jumping into a cesspit.

Yuck! Especially since they still haven't swept out those rushes. The floor is practically steaming by now. It's like a damned quagmire. Give it another two days and they'll be harvesting mushrooms from under the tables.

Joris looks up as we enter.

"Where is Lord Galhard?" Roland demands. Joris nods at the door behind the dais, and immediately returns to the sword he's polishing. There's no one else in the room. I suppose Berengar must be upstairs, nursing his injured leg. And Jordan? I wonder if Jordan survived that beating. Let's hope so, for Roland's sake. Fratricide is the last thing Roland needs right now.

He limps to the threshold of Galhard's sleeping chamber, worn and weary, his white tunic as gray as a dishcloth with dirt and sweat. Dust has settled into the lines around his eyes. His bruises are blooming like bouquets of flowers. "My lord?" he says. "May I come in?"

A grunt from behind the door. Roland pushes it open, and here we are in Galhard's room. The smell is foul. Walls black with smoke; corners thick with cobwebs; a floor slippery with spit and candle wax. Frayed hangings on the beautiful carved bed, which looks exactly like a rat's nest: a porridge of blankets and straw and dirty clothes and bread crusts. Galhard is sitting on the only chair, yawning and rubbing his eyes. (Must have been asleep.) He's dressed in the most exquisite ankle-length robe, an angel's robe, of the very finest embroidered blue silk. A jeweled girdle, too. And a woolen cloak as soft as a duckling's down.

He's even combed his hair.

"Oh, it's you, is it?" he growls, glaring at Roland with his rodent's eyes. "I thought you'd gone for good."

"No, my lord." Roland's voice is as cold as steel.

"Better not let Jordan see you. He's armed and dangerous."

"My lord, I've come back here to make a request."

"Well, you'd better hurry. I'm expecting the Morlans some time soon—"

"My lord, owing to your recent expedition, the countryside is no longer safe for people such as Esclaramonde Maury." (Roland doesn't even wait for Galhard to finish his sentence: he just plows on.) "She and her companions are now waiting at the gates, seeking sanctuary within these walls. Her own farm is not defensible."

"Esclaramonde Maury?" Galhard wrinkles his brow. "Who's she?"

"My lord—"

"Hold on. You don't mean that loudmouthed holy woman?"

"She's not—"

"Damn your eyes, Roland." Galhard's face is twitching. His hand is unsteady. Could he be suffering from a hangover? "I told you before, that woman's not setting foot in this castle again."

"My lord, Mistress Maury and her friends are under your jurisdiction. You owe her your protection, my lord."

"That doesn't mean I owe her a bed. She can lodge with someone in the village." Galhard lurches to his feet and stands for a moment, massaging his temples with both hands. He makes a face as if he's just bitten into a lemon.

Yes, that's a hangover, all right. And it couldn't have happened to a more deserving soul.

"Where's the wine?" he mutters, casting around for something to drink. But Roland isn't about to admit defeat.

"My lord, you do owe her a bed," he says very quietly, but with great force. "If it wasn't for your actions, she wouldn't be here in the first place."

"My actions?" Galhard sounds grumpy. "You're the one who brought her here."

"And you're the one who desecrated the Abbey of Saint Jerome!" The blood rises in Roland's checks as he steps forward. Uh-oh. Keep it cool, Roland. Please don't lose your temper, not now. "You're the one who fouled Christ's sanctuary, my lord! You're the one who shed the blood of God's faithful! When the lords of Montferrand have seen what you've done, they will lay waste to your lands and pour out their fury upon it!"

Galhard snorts. "I'd like to see them try," he says, stooping to pick up a jug. But it's empty.

"Indeed, they will try!" Roland exclaims. "You know they will! That's why the innocent must be protected—"

"Rubbish." God preserve us. Galhard's getting impatient now. "Why should Roquefire de Montferrand bother with a bunch of crazy women? He's got more important things to worry about."

"That's not true—"

"And even if he does rape a couple of them, so what? It won't do any harm. It'll probably do them

277

some good, especially that loudmouthed mosquito in charge. What she needs is a damned good roll, if you ask me. In fact, she'd probably enjoy it."

Oh, you filthy pus-bag—

"How dare you?!" Roland, exploding. "How dare you—you—stinking worm—dung-head—take that back, you scorpion! Disgusting, filthy, stupid—"

"What?" Galhard. Through his teeth. "What did you say?"

"Animal! You're an animal!" (God, Roland, no. No. Please don't say it.) "You're brainless! You smell like a pig! You make me ill—you—you're not even a man! You're the whore of Babylon, drunk with the blood of the saints! You're the Devil's spawn, and you'll go to the Devil with all your bloody deeds, you verminous scum, you excrement, may God smite you down in your corruption—"

Galhard springs. He grabs Roland's surcoat with both hands and slams him against the wall.

"Shut up!"

"Louse! Bile! Peasant—"

"SHUT UP!"

Whoomp! Roland buckles—punched in the belly—Galhard grabs his hair—

God preserve us! "Stop! No!"

278

Driving his knee into Roland's forehead.

"No!" You bastard! You maggot! I launch myself at Galhard's waist, and he stumbles, off-balance, caught by surprise. Reeling. "Leave him alone! You slime-bag! Don't you dare touch him!"

Oh, God. Galhard's face. He's going to kill me. Run, Pagan, run! But Roland—I can't leave him—

Ouch! Let go!

"You've got an impudent tongue, boy," Galhard pants. (Ow! Ouch! My wrist!) "It's the sort of tongue I can do without."

Fingers like clamps. Practically pulling my arm from its socket. Kick out; miss; make haste, O God, to deliver me, make haste to help me, O Lord. Roland groaning on the floor, doubled up, blood streaming from his nose.

Galhard's grip on my neck. Help! What's he doing? God, he's strong. "Let go! Let go, you scum-bucket!"

Crack! Stars. What—? Who—? He must have hit me . . . and this is the bed. The bed? On my stomach, on the bed. Can't get up—something heavy—and Galhard's fingers knocking against my teeth.

What's he—?

"If you can't use this tongue properly, you don't

279

deserve to have it at all," he hisses. Groping in my mouth. Mouth. Tongue. Tongue! Help!

"NAAGH!"

Biting hard—hold on. He shouts. Yes! Salty blood. Don't let go. *Whoomp!*

Shock. Darkness. Fading to pink. Eyes all blurred, jaw numb. Feels like a blow to the side of my head. The taste of his fingers—the flash of a blade—

No!

"Naagh!" Fight, Pagan, fight! Bite and scratch and scream and scream—

"I'll kill you!" Roland's voice, faint, far away. "If you hurt him, I'll kill you! I'll tear you apart!"

Help! Help me! I can't even—he's pulling my tongue—*Roland! ROLAND!*

"My lord!"

Jordan. It's Jordan's voice. Galhard freezes.

"What is it?" he gasps.

"The Morlans have arrived, my lord."

"The Morlans?" Galhard's weight shifts.

"They're crossing the bridge now."

A pause. Galhard's heavy breathing. My own heart, pounding in my ears.

"My lord, I really don't think bloodstains would suit the occasion." Jordan, speaking calmly and quietly. "You don't want to ruin your best gown."

Galhard releases my tongue. My tongue! It's still there! Hallelujah.

He climbs off.

"Tell Berengar to come down," he declares. "Find Germain. Get your wife. Hurry."

"Yes, my lord."

Footsteps. Can I move now? Raising my head. Oh, God, oh, God. Shivering so hard that I can barely see straight.

A hand on my shoulder.

"Are you all right?" Must be Jordan's hand. Look around and there he is, beside me. Peering down through a monumental black eye. "Are you hurt?"

Can't speak to say no. My tongue's still in shock. Shaking my head, by way of an answer.

"Are you sure?"

Of course I'm sure. Roland. Where's Roland? Is he bad? Pushing myself upright, but my knees are like cotton. Have to sit down.

Have to stop shivering.

"You'll be all right." Jordan's hand, cool and dry on the back of my neck. "But you'd better go before my father returns. Take yourself off somewhere, and keep your head down for a few days." Squeezing gently. "He's always like this when he's got a hangover, not to mention a toothache."

Roland. Poor Roland. Creeping across the floor, one hand jammed under his bloody nose, breathing through his mouth in sharp little gasps.

"Oh, my lord. My lord, is it serious?" Please, please don't let him be hurt. Don't let him die. Oh, of course he won't die. Of course he won't. Don't be stupid, Pagan. Suddenly Jordan releases my neck.

"Get out," he says. "Just get out, fast." And he leaves the room slowly, using the wall for support, stiff and pale and rather tense around the middle. Of course! He's been injured, too.

No wonder he hasn't even looked at Roland.

"Pagan." Roland's voice, weak and breathless. His fingers, closing around mine. "I'm so sorry. I'm so sorry, Pagan."

"My lord—"

"I shouldn't have brought you. I shouldn't have said those things. I don't know what happened. . . ." Closing his eyes, tightly.

"My lord, are you hurt? Is it bad? You should lie down."

"No," he says. "No, we can't stay here. Can you stand? Can you help me up?"

"Yes, my lord."

"Then we must warn Esclaramonde. We must get them out of this place." Clutching my hand the way a drowning man would clutch at a spar. "We must take them to the village. Before my father— before he—before—"

Yes, yes, I understand. You don't have to explain. I know exactly what you're talking about.

After all, I've still got the taste of Galhard on my tongue.

‡CHAPTER TWENTY-THREE‡

Clack, clack. Clack, clack. Clack, clack. The sound of weavers in the next room.

Curse them. What time is it? Open one eye to squint at the cracks in the shutters, and find myself looking at Roland instead. He's sitting up, fully dressed, with a boot in one hand.

What's he doing? Is is time for breakfast?

"M-my lord."

He winces as he bends down. His face looks like a cockpit, all dried blood and feathers. What did he do to his pillow last night? Chew a hole in it?

"Good morning, Pagan. I hope you slept well."

"You're up."

"Yes, but you can stay in bed if you want to." He tries, unsuccessfully, to smile: his cracked lip prevents him from managing anything more than a grimace. "You deserve a day in bed."

"You're the one who should be in bed, my lord. You're not well."

"Don't concern yourself, Pagan. I won't be going far."

Well, that's good, because you certainly won't be getting very far, in your condition. Look at your poor nose, smeared all over your face. Blazing like a sunset. And those stiff, fumbling fingers. "Here, my lord, let me do that."

"I can do it."

"My lord, you look terrible. You look as if you've been dragged all the way from Jerusalem." (Throwing off my blanket. Reaching for my clothes. Ouch! My head!) "Please lie down. What's the hurry?"

"I want to make sure they're all right," he rejoins. "Who?"

"Esclaramonde and her friends."

Ah, of course. Esclaramonde. Who else? Watching him bite his lip as he tugs at his other boot. Every movement seems to cause him pain. "My lord, they'll be perfectly all right. Why shouldn't they be? It's a big house. That baker is a decent

285

man. If he didn't want them there, he would have said so." Looking around at our tiny room, with its damp, whitewashed walls. "They've probably done better than we have."

"Nevertheless, I want to make certain." And he stands up slowly, as if he's afraid that one of his legs is going to fall off.

"Please, my lord, let me go."

"No."

"But I'm getting dressed now! I'll be ready in an instant!"

"You can follow me when you've done your chores."

"My lord, wait." He pauses on the threshold, a fold of butter-colored curtain in his hand. You can hear the clacking of the looms: it's enough to drive you crazy.

"What?" he says.

"My lord, you ought to know—I mean—it's about Esclaramonde—"

"What?" He's frowning now.

"My lord, I—I don't think you heard Garsen yesterday." (Come on, Pagan, spit it out.) "She was telling me what the heretics think about marriage. They don't like it, my lord. They say it's a sin, because it leads to children. And a child is just another soul condemned to the sorrows of this world." God preserve us, but this is difficult. My ears are burning up. "I just thought you ought to know, my lord. Before anything . . . well . . . happens."

Waiting. And waiting. A long, long silence. Roland's eyes freeze over. Every vestige of expression leaves his battered face.

"What makes you think I have the slightest interest in such heretical falsehoods?" he says at last. He's convincing, but not convincing enough. Come on, Roland, you can't fool me.

"My lord. I'm not blind, you know."

Another long pause. I can tell he's struggling. Somewhere deep inside, he's struggling. Please, Roland. Why don't you talk to me? You *never* talk to me. Well, hardly ever. Once or twice, perhaps. And even then it's like pulling teeth.

"I'm going to wash," he declares. "Then I'll be visiting the baker's house. You may follow if you so choose."

Very well, then, don't talk. Keep it all bottled up inside, and see what good it does you. No wonder you're always so miserable. How can I help if you won't let me?

Watching as he slips through the curtain, still limping (though not as badly as before). There's a lull in the noise from the next room: must be getting him breakfast, I suppose. Mmmm, breakfast. I could do with a bite of breakfast myself, after I've combed my hair. Providing, of course, that I can actually persuade old Ermengoaud to give me some. Ermengoaud the Amiable. Service with a scowl. Not that you can really blame him, I suppose. After all, we have thrown his brother out of this room. It's not much of a room, of course, but it's better than sleeping on a pile of wool bales in the shed outside. And it's not as if Ermengoaud's letting us stay here out of the kindness of his heart. If Roland's family didn't have procuration rights over half the village—if people like Ermengoaud weren't forced to provide free bed and board for the family's guests at least three times a year—then I daresay Ermengoaud and his wife wouldn't waste spit on us.

Well, maybe that's not quite true. They'd probably give Roland a place to sleep. But they wouldn't let someone like me lick the wool grease off their shuttles. Oh, yes, it's the same old story. They won't even risk handing me anything: they always put it down first, and wait for me to pick it up. They won't look at me. They won't talk to me.

They won't let their little girls stay in the same room.

Well, damn them, anyway. Why should I care what they think? They're just a bunch of stodgy, bog-faced weavers with a ten-word vocabulary. They wouldn't know a joke if it walked through the door and introduced itself. God knows what they do when they're not weaving. Sit around watching their fingernails grow, I daresay.

"Master."

Whoops! And that's one of them, speaking through the curtain.

"Uh—yes?"

Aurencha pushes the curtain aside. She has hands like bunches of carrots, and the mournful, drooping features of a lymer hound, so heavy and despondent and pendulous that they look as if they're going to slide off her face onto the floor at any moment.

"Lord Jordan is here," she announces, and disappears again. What—? Who—?

Suddenly he's on the threshold. Tall. Bruised. Smelling of grass and dogs and damp earth.

"Hello, Pagan." He looks uncharacteristically serious. "May I sit down?"

There's hardly room to move in here. He squeezes past and drops onto Roland's bed. Looks as if he's been overdoing things. His forehead is damp, his color unhealthy. The black eye has faded a little.

"I thought I'd catch you on your way to the horses," he says. "It's the first thing you do every morning, isn't it? But when I saw Roland leaving the house by himself, it occurred to me that I might just be able to talk to you here."

Talk to me? About what? Oh, I know.

"My lord, I want to thank you for what you did yesterday." (Of course, how could I forget? You maggot-bag, Pagan.) "If it hadn't been for you, I wouldn't be able to talk. I owe you a great debt of gratitude. Please tell me if there's anything I can do in return." But he shakes his head, smiling.

"What I did for you, Pagan, is no more than what you did for me." A long, blue stare. What's he talking about? I wish he wouldn't smile like that; it makes me nervous. "Don't you remember?" he says.

"I do. It was in a certain room, in the abbey—"

"Oh, that." Sudden vision of Jordan, cringing on the floor, with an iron lamp stand crashing down.

"Yes, that," he murmurs. "You owe me nothing,

290

Pagan. Nevertheless, I must admit that I've come here this morning to make a request."

"Oh." (What's he after? Nothing tricky, I hope. It's going to be damned awkward, if he wants something from Roland.) "You may not know this, but I hold my own lands," he continues. "A fort and a hamlet, north of here, in the foothills of the Black Mountains. Berengar will have Bram, so I was given Suriac."

Well, congratulations, but what's that got to do with me?

"I'm telling you this because I want you to know that I don't have to stay in Bram." His wide, unblinking stare, glued to my face like dough. "I spend a good deal of time in the mountains, and in Carcassonne. My family has interests in Carcassonne."

Uh-oh. Don't tell me this is what I think it is. Please, God, don't let him say it.

"So if you decide to enter my service," he concludes softly, "you wouldn't be stuck here in Bram. I'd make sure of that."

Damn me, he said it. What am I going to do? I can't just—he'll be furious—this is so difficult!

"I'm asking you to enter my service, Pagan."

291

"My lord, I—my lord, it's a great honor. Truly. But I can't, I just can't."

"Why not?"

"My lord, Foucaud is far more efficient than I am. I've seen the way he looks after your clothes—"

"Damn my clothes." Intensely. "I don't want you to look after my clothes."

"Then why do you want me?"

He leans forward, his skin pale against his charcoal-gray tunic.

"I want you because you're smart," he replies. "I want you because you're funny. I want you because you've seen the world and you've laughed at it. Oh, yes, I know the way you laugh, Pagan. I know exactly what's going on inside your head. Why? Because I know you. I know you so well, we're like two halves of the same person. I can read you better than you can read any book." Almost whispering, now. "Roland doesn't understand you. He can't protect you. He doesn't even appreciate you. You're an ornament, a treasure. You're educated, you're astute, and you're a delight to the eye. Stay with me, Pagan. You won't regret it, I swear."

God.

He's a Ganymede.

Yes. No. Yes. Oh, yes. He's a Ganymede, all

right. A hare. A mule. A boy-chaser. There's no mistaking . . . I've seen that look before, in the Mount Sion bathhouse. It all makes sense. His attention, his help, his kindness, everything.

But no, it can't be. He's married! Except, well, that doesn't mean a lot, does it? What about the shopkeeper who approached me that time on the Street of Flowers? I know for a fact that he was married. And he was still dragging men into bed with him.

"Please, Pagan, just think about it. Think about your future."

Oh, hell, this is awful. But how could I have guessed? He certainly hasn't made a point of it, has he? I bet no one else has realized—except his wife, perhaps.

What the hell am I going to say?

"My lord, you do me too much honor." (Careful, Pagan, be very, very careful.) "If I was still in a city garrison, it would be different. But Lord Roland is my lord now. I couldn't leave him, not unless he told me to. Surely you must see that? It would be wrong."

At last he lowers his gaze. Looks down at his hands, which lie open in his charcoal-gray lap. Studies his bruised knuckles.

"I'm sorry, my lord. I'm really very sorry." I am, too. I'm sorry he's so lonely that he's come to this. Who knows what kind of a life he's led? People like him don't have it easy. I've known a few of them in Jerusalem, and all I can say is: O give thanks unto the Lord, for His mercies to me endureth forever. Their road is a hard and dangerous one.

Jordan rises abruptly.

"Well," he snaps, "a fool hath no delight in understanding, I suppose."

"My lord—"

"You're ten kinds of fool, Pagan. I never realized it, until now." He turns on his heel; pauses; turns back. "And I don't know what Roland thinks he's doing, but if he continues to court destruction as he has been, you may not be in his service for much longer. Just be aware that if he does manage to commit suicide, my offer still stands." His expression is chilly, disdainful, but his voice softens as he finishes. "If you need me, you know where I'll be."

He has to stoop to pass through the door, and the curtain swings shut behind him. God preserve us. I hope he doesn't lose his temper over this. I hope he doesn't get marinated and nail Father Puy's head to a crossbeam, or try to poke my eyes out with a burning stick. It's awful to think what might happen, if he decides that he doesn't like me anymore. Maybe I shouldn't have been so—well, so definite.

Collapsing onto Roland's bed, which sways and creaks as if it's about to fall over. What am I going to do now? What are we going to do now? The Crusade's been postponed indefinitely; Roland's become infatuated with a heretical nun; and we seem to be sinking into a slough of petty quarrels and vicious little homicidal expeditions. What a mess. What a complete shambles. Surely there must be more to life? Surely we didn't come all this way just to lose our path in one of the meanest corners of God's creation?

I must be getting old. It all strikes me as so hollow and pointless and miserable.

CHAPTER TWENTY-FOUR

"Pagan!"

"Hmm . . . ?"

"Pagan!"

What? What is it? What's that noise? It sounds like—yes. It is. It's screaming.

Sit up. What's the time? There's just the faintest, palest light creeping through the shutters. Roland's barely visible: his white tunic shimmers in the gloom.

A crash from outside.

"Wake up! Get up! Hurry!"

God preserve us. What's happening? Scramble for my sword. My boots, my shield. Hurry! The sound of hoof-beats thudding past our wall. One—two—five—six horses.

Aurencha bursts into the room.

"My lord!" she wails. "My lord! My lord!"

Roland pushes past her. Through the curtain, toward the front door. Ermengaud's carrying his little daughter: her sister is crying and clutching his leg. Tears glisten in the light of a single candle.

"My lord! Wait! My lord!" Their voices follow us out, pleading, frightened. *Crash!* What was that? Crisp air; the smell of smoke; the first, faint flush of dawn. People scurrying past, half-dressed, dragging children, swinging axes, shouting, fleeing, pounding on doors. "Brigands! Brigands! Run for your lives!"

Brigands?! I don't believe it.

"The stables!" Roland gasps. "Quickly!"

The stables. The horses. Where are they? I'm lost. But Roland knows the way. Pounding along ahead of me, his sword in one hand, his shield in the other. Houses, houses, and hoofbeats behind us. Someone screaming. Turn around, and there they are. Three of them, mounted, each bearing a flaming torch. Shields. Swords. Chain mail. And a white trefoil on the red field of Languedoc.

Those men aren't brigands.

They gallop past; swerve; disappear. What the hell are they doing? Oh, I know. The torches. The smoke. They're looking for something flammable.

Round a corner into a narrow street. Muddy and dark, and the smoke is getting thicker. Roland! Wait! I can't keep up! *Oof!* Get out of the way, you moron!

Stumbling over someone's smashed skull. Oh, God. Up ahead, people fighting. Screams. Thuds. A seething knot of bodies near a doorway, and there it is, that white trefoil, pouncing on a family as each member stumbles out—choking and weeping—to escape the chaos inside. A gray-haired man falls, and is dragged off his own front step. He's dumped. Kicked. Stabbed once. Twice. Three times.

The blade flashes red in the light of the leaping flames.

Thunk! Roland attacks, so fast that you can barely see him move. Leaps forward. One blow, hard across the neck. Blood sprays out, and a trefoil collapses. But there's another—whoops! Roland! Watch out!

Oh, no, you don't.

"Hoi!"

Look! Here I am! Come and get me, crater-face!

He swings wide. (Yah-hah, missed me.) And swings again. Hits my shield. Back you get—back—back—go on—*yes!* His heel hits the stair, and he falls backward. Now! Now!

But he rolls, too quickly.

"Pagan!"

Turn! Strike! Help! A man . . . his red chest . . . thrust in. Hard. The shudder. Pulling out. Stepping back . . .

Blood on my hand. On my sword. The body, squirming at my feet. Cries of pain. Jesus, oh, Jesus.

It was me. I did it. He's there, and I did it.

"Pagan!"

Roland, grabbing my arm. Pulling. Hauling. Wait! Slow down! I can't run this fast. Fall to one knee; dragged up again. This smoke is terrible. My eyes are so sore. And that squealing, that's not human. That's horses. Are we near the stables, then?

"Here! Pagan! In here!"

I recognize this. This is the smith's barn. They obviously haven't found it yet. It's very dim inside, but there's no mistaking the clatter and thump of frightened horses. "Curse it!" Roland pants. "I can't see a thing." He pushes the door wide open, and it screeches across the cobbles. "Hurry, Pagan! Saddle up! I'll guard the entrance."

Right. Where's Fennel? There she is, and there's her bridle, and who's this? A stunted gnome, shivering behind a feed bin. Must be the stable boy.

"You! Yes, you! See that horse? I want to ride it. The harness is over there." (Come on, you fool!) "Move! Hurry!"

Calm down, Fennel. Calm down, girl. She tosses her head as I wipe my sword on my tunic. Shhh, take it easy. Sheathe my sword. Grab her saddle. Throw it across her back, and grope for the girth. My hands are shaking so much that it's hard to join the straps.

"Hurry, Pagan!"

"Yes, my lord, yes."

Damn it! How can I get a grip on this buckle with my fingers all slippery . . . covered in blood . . . warm and wet.

Did I kill him? I must have. I felt—no. Stop. Don't think about it. Just don't think at all. This is no time for thinking.

Wait a moment. That shout. Was that Galhard? Suddenly Roland's beside me, dragging the bridle over Fennels's twitching ears.

"My lord, wait, who are they? Are they—?"

"The Montferrands. Who else?" he replies, and leaps into his saddle. Fennel lurches forward as he

300

drums at her flanks with his heels. Heading for the barn door.

What the hell does that stable boy think he's doing? Seems to be putting my saddle on backward.

"Move, you bog-brain! Get out of the way! I'll do it myself."

"Hurry, Pagan!"

"I'm coming. I'm coming."

But Coppertail's frightened. He won't stand still. "Please, please, calm down, will you?" Now Roland's disappeared. Thanks very much, Roland. Just go off and leave me: I don't care. Where's the bridle? Where's that boy? "Oi! Wait! Where are you going?" (What's his problem?)

Turn around, and there's a trefoil, storming through the barn's back entrance.

Sweet saints preserve us.

Run. Run! Out the front. Into the street. Roland! Where's Roland? Is that him? It certainly looks like Fennel's backside, retreating down the road. But who's that with him? Berengar? "My lord!" Running hard. "My lord! Wait!"

Other people, running. A house, burning. But there's someone on horseback, pursuing a trefoil. Pons! It's Pons! And there's Ademar! Praise the Lord, we're on the offensive. "Pons!" (Cough, cough.) "Pons! Pons!" He doesn't hear. Charges off down an alley with his lance tucked under his armpit. This is chaos. Chaos. What am I going to do?

Stop. Think. A smoky haze hangs low over the peaked roofs. Stone walls everywhere, all looking the same. A dry water trough and a stack of firewood, just waiting to be lit. Roland. I've got to find Roland. I'm a moving target, if I don't. Or perhaps I should make my way back to the castle? That's if I can actually find the castle. I've completely lost my bearings here. All these smelly little streets look alike. And the crowds don't seem to be heading in one direction, either.

A woman staggers into view, dripping blood. Dazed. Weeping. God, this is iniquitous. How could they do that? How can I help? Perhaps if I take her to the church, or the castle—

Suddenly, the sound of hoofs and raised voices.

"Look out! Mistress! Over here, quickly!"

But she keeps plodding along, like a sleep-walker. Get out of the way, you fool! Can't you hear they're coming? Darting out to drag her back. Quick! Quick! Against the wall! A skidding horse, rounding the corner, stumbling, recovering, galloping past with blood on its flanks and a trefoil in the saddle. His open mouth; staring eyes; blood-soaked tunic. That man's in retreat.

There's another, and another. Flashing by like birds, kicking up the mud, and there's Jordan! It's Jordan! And Galhard! And—

"My lord!"

Running after Roland. Left turn. Right turn. Left turn. The sound of a battle horn. Erupting into the village square, under showers of ash, and it's hard to see what's going on in this poor light, through the veils of smoke, but it's a skirmish. Definitely a skirmish. The whirlwind of plunging horses moves this way, that way, and somebody falls—a trefoil—knocked off his saddle by Jordan's lance. He rolls between the lashing hoofs. A sword blade rings as it hits the grounds. But where's Roland? Ah, there he is. Plowing into his opponent like a headwind, like somebody chopping wood, pushing him toward the others—oh! I see now. I see what's happening. The trefoils form a tight little knot, as Jordan and Galhard and Roland circle them, prodding and pounding, with Joris and Aimery in support, exactly like a team of hunters with a stag at bay.

Suddenly the trefoils surge in a single direction, trying to break through. Galhard is knocked sideways, but manages to retain his seat. A cry of pain from one of the trefoils: he sags against his horse's neck, wounded somehow, letting his lance drop from nerveless fingers. Nevertheless, he keeps going. They all do. Pounding along, straight across the square, straight toward me, with Jordan and Galhard and Roland in pursuit.

Move, Pagan! Out of the way!

"My lord! Wait! My lord!"

This time he hears. This time he sees. Reining poor Fennel in so sharply that she rears like an unbroken colt.

"I can't stop!" he pants. "Find Esclaramonde!"

"My lord—"

"Look after her!"

And off he shoots. So now I have to find Esclaramonde! Easier said than done, Roland. And what am I supposed to do when I find her, overwhelm a savage mob of Montferrand supporters with my fingernails? Don't you care what happens to me? I can't believe that you've just left me alone in the middle of this bloodbath!

Wandering westward, toward the baker's house. It's very quiet, all of a sudden. The streets seem to be deserted. No marauding trefoils, no fleeing villagers. Occasionally, the sound of someone moaning behind a barred door. Where is everybody? Have the trefoils retreated? Perhaps they have. Perhaps it was a flying raid: in and out fast, before Galhard could collect his wits. A dead goose, smeared all over the ground. Smashed furniture. Doors hanging ajar, vomiting trails of trampled clothes and squashed food and bed linen. The heat growing more intense, as a burning roof appears around a corner, crackling and spitting. The clouds of black smoke, rolling up into a pall that blocks out the sky.

No, not that way. There must be another approach. Turn left, and right. A body, blocking my path. Dead? Stopping, unsteadily, to feel for a pulse. The hand is very dry. Yes, he's dead. Can't do much about that. Can't do much about anything. Stumbling forward—so tired—coughing and coughing, my eyes wet and raw. I feel like a ghost. A ghost in an empty village. Where are they all? Have they run off to the castle, do you think? But someone must be here, because that's the sound of grieving. A wail that grows louder, and softer, and louder again. "No, no . . . no no *no* . . ." It's quite close, too. But where? I can't see. Peering through the haze, my footsteps slapping against dead earth.

A dark figure, crouched just ahead. No, not one figure. Two. And another, curled up on the ground. The terrible keening rises above them, boring into my skull, and I feel as if I'm going to faint, I feel sick, no, it can't be, but it is—Garsen's face, turned toward me, contorted with rage and despair: "Look what you did!" she screams. "You! It was you! All of you!"

No. Oh, no. Not Esclaramonde. Please God, no. Just a glimpse—her white face—her bloody lips—half-closed eyes—

"She tried to stop them," Helis sobs. "She ran out . . . she grabbed the reins . . ."

"Sister. Oh, Sister, Sister . . ."

"They went right over her. The men with the torches. Every one of them. . . ."

Her long hair, splashed across the dirt, sticky with blood.

Oh, God, oh, God. It can't be true. Not this. Not her. I can't look, I can't bear it. I can't bear it!

"Sister. Oh, Sister . . ."

Get me out of here. I can't stand this anymore. This is it. No more. I've had enough. Just get away, away from that moaning. Run down the street. Run away from the corpse: her corpse, his corpse, the man I killed. You killed a man, Pagan. At last, you've killed a man. You stuck a sword in his guts, and you pulled it out again. You wiped off his guts on your tunic. His guts are still there, on your hands and your legs. He's dead, now, like her—like Esclaramonde—oh, Roland. Help me. Help me, help me, what am I going to do?

"Pagan!"

Turn, and there he is. Galloping up a side street. Where did he come from? Why is he here? If I tell him, he'll kill me. He'll die. No, I can't do it.

"Pagan! Stop! Where are you—?"

Run. Run! Hoofbeats, gaining. Suddenly he's in front of me. Leaps down, grabs my arm, both arms, panting. "Pagan! It's me!" (A shake.) "What's wrong? Are you hurt? Why are you crying?"

Oh, Roland. Oh, Roland.

"They've gone, Pagan, there's nothing to fear. We chased them out."

No, no, you don't understand. Pointing up the street, but I can't talk—the tears—I can't—

His hands tighten on my arms.

"Esclaramonde," he says. Suddenly he's taken off, he's running, back up the street, straight to where I pointed, toward Garsen, toward Esclaramonde.

No, Roland, no! It will kill you! "Roland! Don't look!" But he's almost there, he's slowing, he's seen—he must have seen—and he swerves, blindly. He turns away. He staggers in helpless circles. He presses his hands to his mouth and he sways and shuts his eyes and falls to his knees. Gasping behind his hands. Choking behind his hands. Folded up, now, with his forehead almost striking the earth in front of him.

"Roland—Roland—"

But he straightens and his lungs fill and he screams behind his hands, screams in agony—I can't bear it—don't, Roland, don't, you're going to kill me, and he's groaning, now, groaning as if he's being stabbed, and the tears spill down his bruised cheeks.

Roland, oh, Roland. Feeling him shudder like a great tree under the blow of an axe as I hug him, try to comfort him, but I can't, it's impossible, it's so bad that Helis has to put her hands to her ears, that Garsen's stopped moaning and started praying. "Roland, don't—Roland, don't, don't, please. . . ." All I can do is hold him, my poor Roland, pierced to the bone by every one of his muffled cries because his face is buried in my chest, and he's howling straight through my rib cage, clinging so hard that I can barely breathe. Slowly the howls become words; the words become intelligible.

"Pagan, Pagan . . ."

I'm here, Roland. I'm here. I always will be.

✢CHAPTER TWENTY-FIVE✢

It's not a bad place to be buried, if you have to be buried in unconsecrated ground. At least half a mile from the nearest church, of course, but that wouldn't matter to Esclaramonde. Why should it? She'd like the flowers, too. Golden buds everywhere, with a spray of purple iris near her feet. An oak tree shielding her from the northern winds. And Garsen's clump of rosemary, planted in the freshly turned soil.

A dead leaf flutters down. That's three dead leaves already. Soon her whole grave will be covered. The earth will dry out, the grass will come, and only the neat pile of rocks will remain. But they won't be disturbed because it's very peaceful out here. Very lonely. In fact it's a little too lonely. Oh, Lord, please don't let her be lonely. Please don't make her suffer. Even if she was wrong, she had a good heart. Think of the Magdelene: the Magdelene's sins were many, and they were forgiven because she loved much. Surely it would be the same with Esclaramonde?

Garsen, kneeling, with her head covered. Garsen won't speak to us now. Helis will, but she didn't last long. Had to be taken back to the village by Estolt after she collapsed at the graveside. Grazide, sniffing. Braida, holding Othon's hand. All completely silent, as a gentle breeze tugs at their shawls and hems and loose wisps of hair, and the oak dips above us, and the speckles of shadow rearrange themselves on Esclaramonde's grave.

As for Roland, I can hardly bear to look at him. Such a difference, in just one day: it's as if he's being eaten away from the inside. Looking ten years older. And moving so slowly, so clumsily, like an invalid. Burrowing into himself behind a wall of glazed eyes and silence. Starting to do something, then losing the will. Trailing off into a motionless trance, until somebody jogs his elbow. Lying curled up in bed, with his arms folded across his ribs to stop his heart from breaking.

Kneeling there now, lost and speechless. What am I going to do? Everything's in chaos, and my clothes still smell of smoke and blood. (Blood. Don't think about it.) Coppertail's been killed. Our saddlebags were looted. And then there's Roland. How can he travel when he's in such a state? I still have to steer him through every door.

Be merciful unto me, O God, be merciful unto me; for my soul trusteth in Thee, in the shadow of Thy wings will I make my refuge, until these calamities be overpast.

Suddenly, the sound of footsteps. *Crackle, crackle. Crunch, crunch.* Seems to be coming from the other side of the copse. Will anyone notice? Yes. Othon's heard; he looks around. Braida gives a little squeak and stands up, trembling. Garsen's gone pale, but doesn't move.

Should I draw my sword, or would that be disrespectful? Esclaramonde would never have allowed it, I know.

"Someone's coming, my lord." Touching Roland's shoulder. "My lord? Someone's coming."

He looks up, dreamily, his thoughts far away. Gradually his eyes begin to focus. There's a rustle of leaves, and the sharp crack of a stick breaking.

"Who's there?" Garsen demands. Roland rises to his feet. Grazide stops sniffing.

But it's only Jordan.

"Ah, Roland." He emerges from a tangle of undergrowth, the hem of his tunic catching on burrs and thorns and clawing branches. He looks immensely tired. "I've been searching for you everywhere."

"What do you want?" Roland says hoarsely. (He hasn't spoken in hours.)

"Just a quick word. It won't take long."

"I have nothing to say to you."

"Lord Galhard sent me. This wasn't my own idea."

Roland hesitates. He's still in a fog, though it seems to be clearing. His brother sounds bored and irritable.

"Lord Galhard wants to know if you would consider joining our planned attack on Montferrand," Jordan continues, and all at once Garsen loses her temper. Her angry tones cut across the conversation. "Go away! Both of you!" she cries. "You desecrate this peace! You defile this mourning! How dare you come here with your bloody swords and your corrupt hearts? Go away!"

Jordan smiles, but he doesn't even look at her. His eyes are fixed on Roland.

"Lord Galhard," he finishes, "seems to think that you might have some personal motive for wanting revenge."

God preserve us. How did they—? Quick glance at Roland, who catches his breath.

"Revenge?" he mutters, and somehow he's come alive again. Somehow he's inhabiting his face again. "Is that what you think I want? Revenge?"

"You're mistaken. I don't think anything, myself. I'm merely a messenger."

"Then take a message back to Lord Galhard. Tell him I'm leaving. Tell him I'm finished with all this." A pause, as Roland swallows some emotion. "Tell him to forget that I ever existed."

"Don't worry, he will."

"And tell him—tell him that he who does violence to his brother, does violence to himself. Tell him that."

The brothers lock eyes across Esclaramonde's grave. Jordan isn't smiling anymore. His expression is guarded and somber.

"Very well," he says at last. "I'll pass on that message." His gaze shifts to the blood-spattered squire who's trying to make himself as small as possible in Roland's shadow (without much success). "What about you, Pagan? Have you changed your mind?"

"Uh, no. No, my lord. I'm sorry."

"So am I. I only hope you'll live to regret it." He turns back to Roland. "In God's name," he says quietly, "look after him. Just look after him, will you?"

And off he goes. Head bowed, watching his feet, still a bit stiff around the middle.

I wish I knew how to feel about him.

"My lord!"

He stops. Waits. But doesn't swing around.

"Don't worry, my lord, I can look after myself."

No reply. Suddenly Roland tugs at my arm. What? What is it? You want to go? Jordan's moving again, disappearing into the bushes. Roland strikes out in the opposite direction. Praise God, he seems to be functioning at last. Making decisions and carrying them through.

I can feel Garsen's glare sizzle on our backs.

"My lord." (Where are you going?) "This isn't the way to the village."

"I know. I want to talk to you."

Talk to me? What does that mean? Grasshoppers springing away as we crush the turf underfoot. Low branches tweaking my hair. Does he want to talk about Esclaramonde? About our plans? I hope it's not Jordan. I don't want to talk about Jordan.

Right through a thicket, with Roland ahead of me. Shielding my face from the slapping bushes. Ouch! Thorns. Prickles. The whir of tiny wings as we flush a bird from its hiding place. Roland's footsteps: *crunch, crunch, crunch*. Uneven ground, full of rocks and disguised holes. Skirting a tree trunk.

"My lord? Where are we going?"

"Somewhere private."

Whoops! Watch that log! Clambering over it: slipping on a fan of yellow fungus. What about here? We could stop here. But he plows on, straight into the wall of leaves up ahead. This is ruining my stockings, Roland; they're beginning to look like a goat's fleece.

"Here," he says, and stops (so that I almost run straight into his back). "Careful. Watch your feet."

Look down, and it's a hole. A gigantic, overgrown hole, with walls of loose rubble and a pool of stagnant water at the bottom.

"What's this?"

"I don't know."

"Is it an old quarry?"

"Perhaps. It's been here a long time." Roland

crouches at the edge of the slope. "Sit down, Pagan."

"How deep is the water?"

"Deep enough. Please sit down."

Finding myself a seat on a rock. It's very warm and quiet. Insects hover above the still, murky pool.

Roland takes a deep breath.

"I've come to a decision, Pagan. About our future."

Here it comes. I knew it was coming. He's examining a little tuft of weeds near his right foot. Frowning down at it. Fingering the minute pink blossoms.

"I doubt if you realize how important you are to me," he says at last. "I want you to know that. After what happened yesterday—now that it's finished—there's no one more important than you. No one. I don't know what I would have done without you, Pagan." He begins to pull at the little flowers, wrenching them from the soil, crushing them in his hands. "And that's what makes it so difficult."

Why? What do you mean? What's difficult? What are you talking about?

"Perhaps you don't remember, about a year ago, when I mentioned something about the Abbey of

317

Saint Jerome." (He still won't look at me.) "I told you that I went to the previous Abbot, when I was sick to the heart, and begged for a place behind the abbey walls."

"Yes, of course I remember."

"But he told me that Christendom couldn't spare a knight like me. He sent me to Jerusalem, to fight the Infidel. He said that it was my duty to God."

"Yes, my lord, I remember every word."

"Pagan—" he begins, and pauses. Spit it out, Roland. Tell me. Talk to me. "Bloodshed is not the way to God, Pagan. I know that. No murderer shall ever have eternal life."

"But you're not a murderer!"

"Oh, yes, I am. And I've known it all along . . . it's been so hard. . . ." He's gasping a little, as if it's hurting him to speak. "My mother never wanted me to live by the sword. She said that it wouldn't bring me salvation, and she was right. She was always right, about everything. She wanted me to enter the church. When she—when she died . . ." A long, long pause. "When she died," he continues at last, "I tried to follow her wishes. I did try. I just didn't try hard enough. And now I—you see, Pagan, I—"

"You want to become a monk."

"Yes."

So that's it. That's it. I should have known.

"Not here," he continues, in a breathless voice. "Not at the abbey. Somewhere else. A small, humble place. And this time nothing will stop me, nothing and no one. Except you, perhaps."

Me?

"I know how you hate monasteries, Pagan. I know how you ran away from your monastery in Bethlehem, and I wouldn't want that to happen again. You shouldn't be forced into a life that you don't want to lead." Finally he looks up. Presenting his swollen cheek, his scabs, his bruises. "I can't tell you what to do, because I don't believe I truly have that right anymore. But I can offer you a choice. You have so many gifts that I'm sure you'd be welcome anywhere."

Oh, Roland.

"If I took you to Carcassonne," he adds, "and spoke to Commander Folcrand, he would make you a Templar sergeant immediately. My recommendation would be enough."

"My lord—"

"Or you could join the Knights Hospitaller. There'd be no objection to that. I just — I don't — I realize that Jordan made you an offer, Pagan."

(Oh, hell. I knew it, I knew we'd come to this.) "Maybe I haven't done justice to him, in the past. Maybe I've been blind. I know there's a kind of ancient wound—a poison—that lies between my heart and his, and I know I can't tell you what to do, but I pray that you won't decide to stay with him, Pagan. This place is a pit of vipers. I'd be so afraid for you if you stayed here."

"My lord—"

"I just want you to be happy. Safe and happy."

"My lord, I'm safe and happy with you." In God's name, Roland, why do you even ask? "Where you go, I'll go."

"But if I become a monk—"

"If you become a monk, I can become a monk. Or at least a monastery servant."

He doesn't look very pleased. Knitting his brows. Biting his lips. Scraping a hole in the dirt with his heel. What's the matter, Roland? Don't you want me?

"I feel as if I'm forcing you into something—"

"No, my lord, never. Things have changed. I've changed. I don't . . . I . . . you see I'd never killed anyone . . . not before yesterday. . . ." (Oh, no. No. Stop. Don't think.)

"Pagan? What's wrong?"

320

The slimy blood on my hand. The shudder. The jerk. The awful, deathly moans.

"Pagan. What is it?"

"I killed a man! I killed him!" Oh, God. God help me. God forgive me, forgive my sin, I can't bear it, I can't, I can't. I'm cursed from the earth, which hath opened her mouth to receive my brother's blood. "I'm damned! I'm a murderer!"

"Pagan—"

"I can't—I can't do it—no. Never. Never again."

"Shhh. It's all right. You'll be all right."

"Oh, God, oh, God."

Gulping for breath. The salty taste of tears. Roland's hand on my back, up and down, up and down. "God knows your heart, Pagan." His gentle voice. "God will forgive you."

But how can He, when I can't forgive myself? Now I have this stain on my soul forever. The mark of Cain, and I'll never wash it off.

"Pagan, please don't cry. Please. We have a path, now, a true path." Scrubbing at my face with the corner of his cloak. "Dry your eyes, Pagan. I want you to witness this."

Witness what? What are you doing? He stands up, slowly, and the little loose pebbles roll out from under his feet. They tumble down into the pit, with a patter like raindrops. The folds of his cloak billow in the breeze.

He draws his sword.

Help! What's he doing? A blinding flash—a glitter of gold—as he lifts the blade higher and higher, over his head, leaning back with all his weight on his right foot, and his left arm stretched out in front of him.

He throws.

The heavy sword takes flight. Whirling. Sparkling. Up into the air like a silver bird, like an arrow, fiery in the sunshine, and falling, now. Plummeting. Down and down, still catching the light, down past the cascades of gravel and dandelions.

Until it lands, with a *plop*, in the black water. And slowly disappears from sight.

GLOSSARY

alaunt   A fast and savage hunting dog, resembling a greyhound. Its role was to chase and seize a running beast and bring it down.

Baal   The chief male god of the ancient Phoenicians and Canaanites, mentioned in the Bible as a false god

bailey   The courtyard enclosed within the outer, protective walls of a castle

Battle of Hattin   The battle in which the Turkish sultan Saladin conquered the Christian army of Jerusalem, in the summer of 1187

Book of Life   Mentioned in the Bible as the book opened on the Day of Judgment: the dead will be judged by their deeds, which will be written in this book.

Byzantine   Byzantium was the medieval name for the city now known as Istanbul. At the time, its inhabitants (the Byzantines) were generally Orthodox Christians, rather than Catholics.

chandler   A candle maker and seller

chapter house   The room of a monastery in which the monks formally met to discuss monastic business

cloister garth   The open space or courtyard enclosed by the monastic buildings

consolamentum   A blessing practiced by the heretical Cathar sect. The "priest" of the sect would pass the Holy Spirit to another by laying both hands on his or her head. It was usually employed on a deathbed, to ensure salvation.

crupper   The rump of a horse

Feast of the Holy Cross   May 3

Ganymede   A medieval slang word for a homosexual man, derived from the Greek myth about Ganymede, a beautiful boy abducted by the god Zeus

hauberk   A long military tunic, usually of chain mail

Jacobite   A member of a Christian heretical sect established in the sixth century, which took its name from one Jacobus Bardaeus

keep   The innermost and strongest structure or central tower of a castle, serving as a last defense

lymer   The forerunner of the modern bloodhound, large and heavily jowled, with a strong scenting ability

mangonel   A military engine for casting large stones

palliasse   A straw mattress

perpetual anathema   The great curse of the church: excommunicating or condemning a person to eternal damnation

preceptor   The head of a subordinate community of the Knights Templar. A Grand Preceptor traveled from community to community, holding meetings (chapters) and checking up on things.

psalter   The Book of Psalms (from the Old Testament)

quintain   An object mounted on a post or plank, set up as a mark to be tilted at with lances or poles

Saint John's Day   June 24

setier   A medieval produce measurement

surcoat   An outer garment often worn by armed men over their armor

trefoil   A figure representing a three-lobed leaf (a clover leaf)

tonsure   The part of a priest's or monk's head left bare by shaving the hair

Turcopole   In Jerusalem, a locally born, Arabic-speaking soldier hired by the Knights Templar

varlet   An attendant or servant

vassal   In the feudal system, a person holding lands from a superior on conditions of homage or allegiance; a dependent lordship